First published 2012 by Glynn James & Michael Stephen Fuchs - London, UK

ISBN-13: 978-1500239947
ISBN-10: 1500239941

D1736332

A world fallen - under a plague of seven billion walking dead
A tiny island nation - the last refuge of the living
One team - of the world's most elite special operators
The dead, these heroes, humanity's last hope, all have..

ARISEN

.

NOTES FROM THE AUTHORS

GLYNN

I've learned quite a lot in the process of writing these books. The first, of course, being how to work with another writer. I think Michael will agree that when we started we didn't have much of a clue how this was going to happen or even if the two styles would gel. I think they have. At the start we toyed with various collaboration tools and ended up in Google Docs. The conversations we had about the plot, character development – every aspect of the process really – is almost as long as the book itself. The other part of working with another writer was learning about the shock of your plot and story being in someone else's hands. Characters did things I hadn't planned and the storyline twisted and wove in directions that I hadn't even considered. Characters that I didn't even create suddenly had a voice and were shouting. After the initial confusion I sat back and found myself seriously enjoying how the world I had started was unfolding in someone else's mind (Michael's). I really like the way it all went and continue to be in awe. I hope that everyone that reads this agrees.

NOTES FROM THE AUTHORS

MICHAEL

What I said in the Notes in Book One! Plus this: thanks also to Glynn for the complete and total asskicking covers for this series – they put the best possible face on this awesome work. The man is not only an artist with words, but a proper artist as well.

"All that is of the body is as coursing waters, all that is of the soul as dreams and vapours, life a warfare, a brief sojourning in an alien land; and after repute, oblivion."
– Marcus Aurelius

"Generally speaking, the Way of the warrior is resolute acceptance of death."
– Miyamoto Musashi

EVER ON

Andrew Wesley, former corporal with the UK Security Services, and one-time officer in charge of the night watch at the Channel Tunnel entrance in Folkestone, but now of no fixed abode, stood staring out at the night sky. He was off at the very edge of the gently rolling flight deck of the USS *John F. Kennedy*, as it churned the North Atlantic, steaming back toward its place of origin – the New World.

Now a Dead World.

The boat, a floating city really, was an American supercarrier that at one time had been the base of operations for over 80 combat aircraft. Now it held fewer than two dozen. It had simply turned out that air superiority was of no critical importance in the ZA. Also, pilots had gotten a little thin on the ground, in the two years since the fall of human civilization.

The sun was just now rising, and Wesley squinted into it, thinking fitfully about the unnerving events of the last week. There had been the terrifying outbreak in Folkestone, the death of his two rookies, and then the harrowing firefight in the town as an entire battalion of regular infantry had rushed in to quell the rampaging masses of the dead. And after that, the disorientation and vertigo of getting helicoptered out to the *JFK* in the middle of an endless ocean. It had all happened so quickly, there was no time to process any of it.

Now, as he stared into the first light of another unsettling day, Wesley wondered what in hell they were getting themselves into. Word was that North America was completely dead, or rather undead, down to the last person. And here they were sailing straight for it, on what he could only think of as some mad and terribly ill-considered errand. Not that he had yet been given much information on which to form opinions.

A soft sound from behind startled him from his staring contest with the rising sun. It was Captain Martin, his fellow traveler on this perilous and incomprehensible journey.

"Hiding out?" Martin asked, though it was more statement than question. These two had only known each other a tiny stretch of time. And yet they seemed to know each other well, right from their first meeting – when Wesley had watched Martin emerge from an exploding hotel, just a few steps ahead of a herd of slavering corpses.

"Hiding out seemed much the best thing," replied Wesley. "Keeps me out of everyone's way."

Martin laughed, a warm and genuine sound, which considering recent events was a rare and welcome thing.

"Any idea how long before we arrive?" asked Wesley.

"Dunno, I haven't asked," said Martin with a shrug. "No one's talking about it, least of all the spec-ops boys."

"Hmm. They do rather keep things to themselves. You know, I've never been to America."

"Oh?"

"Nope. Never once. And to be honest I'm not sure I'm looking forward to it now."

"I'll second you on that," Martin said, shrugging. "I have actually been a few times. Though I suppose it's going to be rather less amusing this time around. Wouldn't care to brave the queues at DisneyWorld in its probable current state."

Wesley grinned at that, and the two lapsed into silence, both staring at the rising sun as it scattered dazzling flashes across the rough chop of the ocean's surface. There wasn't much beauty left in this world, but Wesley figured this qualified.

He also wondered what was happening back in Britain in the aftermath of the Folkestone incident. Shocked as he had been at the time, Wesley now figured: if it could happen there it could happen anywhere. And if Fortress Britain, the last significant bastion of surviving humanity, was still so vulnerable... well, then what chance did any of them stand? Then again, the odds that any of them on this boat would ever see Britain again were not something Wesley would care to rate. And if the sublime sight of sunlight on the water were all that were left to him... well, he would enjoy it in this moment that he still had left.

"I'm glad you're here," he said, looking across at Martin.

If there was still beauty in this fallen world, and if there could still be friendship, then maybe that was enough.

QUARANTINE

Lt. Colonel Bryan, Royal Army Medical Corps, vascular surgeon of 22 years experience, and ranking medical officer with USOC (the Unified Special Operations Command) at Hereford, flipped the page of the heavy book in his lap. It was the complete plays of Shakespeare, which he figured was as good a way as any to get through the long hours of the ZA. Seemingly longer still were these shifts in the Quarantine Shack, which sat adjacent to the primary helipad. It had to be manned 24/7 by a medical officer. And Colonel Bryan, OC of the base hospital, insisted on taking his shifts just like everyone else.

Hereford, former barracks of the British SAS, was now the home of USOC – the last, best few hundred special operators left, in what was left of the world. It was from here that these real-life superheroes worked to keep alive the last fifty million or so living humans, in what had now become Fortress Britain. It was only the incredible timing of a terrible terrorist attack, two years earlier, and just a few days before the zombie virus reached a tipping point across the world, that caused Britain to cancel all flights and lock down its borders. And it was those precious few days of isolation that allowed them to hunker down against the advancing rampage of the dead. Now, Doc Bryan and the USOC commanders just had to keep Hereford from going the way of virtually all the other military bases around the world – being overrun from within by infected soldiers brought back inside the wire by their brothers in arms.

The Quarantine Shack was a big part of this.

The facility consisted of one small building with two rooms. One of them was a waiting area for the attending doctor. The other was much larger, reinforced, lockable from the outside, and stocked with cots, food, water, limited medical supplies, and various items of minor comfort. Along one edge sat a cage with the sniffing dogs. An enclosed passage led directly from there to the base hospital, making the whole place basically a big conduit there from the helipad. A conduit that could be opened – or locked down and tightly controlled.

Bryan flipped another wispy page. Frankly, what he could only think of as the 16th-century slang of the Bard defeated him. The heavy annotations helped somewhat.

The phone on his desk rang.

"Bryan."

"*Incoming,*" the voice on the other end announced. "*It's Echo team. They're back from over the water, with one litter urgent casualty. ETA five mikes.*"

"Nature of the injury?" Bryan thunked his book shut and pushed it across the desk.

"*Unknown at this time. Stand by.*"

Bryan hung up, dialed the hospital duty desk, and summoned two medical orderlies. They came trotting up within ten seconds, wide-eyed and expectant. Bryan nodded at them gravely, moved to the door that opened on the big room, worked the locks, then stepped inside. Turning again, he nodded to the orderlies through the thick plexiglas.

And they locked him in.

Less than a minute later, Bryan could hear the rotors and jet engines of the incoming helo. Other than pulling on some latex gloves and a face shield, there was really nothing to prepare on this end. Everything was all set up. It always was. He moved to the cages where the two dogs stood alert, sniffing, tails wagging.

"Hullo, lads," Bryan said, palming a couple of treats from the table and feeding them through the bars. "How are we this fine apocalyptic day? Good boys, good boys."

He heard the hurricane-like sounds of the bird flaring outside. A moment later, the outer door banged open, letting in the roiling wind and dust. A lolling and unconscious, or barely conscious, operator was supported from each sides by two others. One of them held an IV bag, the drip from which snaked around them into the casualty's arm. All three were dressed in full battle rattle – bite suits, Kevlar, tactical load-bearing vests, mags, grenades, sidearms, and short swords.

As they lurched in, the wounded man's feet drug

on the floor behind them. He had a thick, blood-soaked bandage wrapped around his neck.

That doesn't look good, thought Bryan. He didn't just mean the seriousness of the injury.

Before he could ask, one of the Echo men said, "It's a ricochet, Doc. *Just a ricochet*." They weren't putting down their burden, but merely angled him toward the exit door.

"Let me examine him," Bryan said. "Lay him down."

The two looked agitated, but complied. "He's bleeding out, Doc," one said as he laid his brother operator down. As they put him on the gurney alongside the cage, the two dogs started going apeshit, barking and snarling.

"He's half-covered in Zulu goo," the other Echo guy said. It was true – there was a lot of gore on the man's armor and particularly his boots. Some of it was black. If it was fresh, and it was, that would set off the dogs.

Gingerly but expertly, Bryan peeled back the bandage. It looked like his right common carotid had been severed. And from the man's color, he'd already lost an enormous amount of blood. The shape of the wound was consistent with a gunshot. It certainly wasn't a bite – though a scratch could conceivably produce something like this.

"See? Like we said. Stray round."

Bryan looked up. "What was the path of the

bullet?" On at least one other documented occasion, a round had passed through a Zulu and into a soldier – with enough organic matter on it to infect the man. It was damned rare – a little like the apocryphal Civil War nurse said to be impregnated by the musket ball that passed through a soldier's teste – but it happened.

"It sparked off a car. We were all on the same side of the street." Frequently, in CQB (close quarters battle), shooters were on all sides of a structure – and moving 100 miles an hour. In those cases, a round passing through a wall or an enemy could be a hazard, hitting a teammate on the other side. But not in this case? Bryan frowned. Could a round have gone through a Zulu, then ricocheted back? Because these guys rarely missed entirely. And could it still carry infectious material?

The casualty convulsed on the litter, spitting up blood and bile. Shock from extreme blood loss. He was in fact bleeding out.

One of the Echo men put pressure on the wound. The other put his hand on his sidearm. "Colonel," the man said through gritted teeth. "Kindly open the door. This man's coming in."

Well, Bryan thought with resignation, *at least he's not holding the gun to my head...* He would just have to take responsibility – not to mention personally sit with the patient every second until he died, or until he recovered.

He made a thumbs-up toward the plexiglas. The

locks clanked, the door banged open, and the two orderlies raced in. They unlocked the wheels on the gurney and raced out and down the hall toward the base hospital. Bryan followed at a trot behind them.

And the dogs carried on barking until they were out of hearing.

STAND FAST

In the wake of the long and disturbing briefing on their upcoming mission to the middle of dead North America, the operators of Alpha, officers and men both, had swung into action with mission prep work. There was a lot of it. The eight-man team was going to parachute directly into Chicago and try to get out with a vaccine developed there by a biotech called NeuraDyne Neurosciences. They were going to HAHO jump out over Lake Michigan, fly in on the prevailing winds, land on top of the target building, and fight their way down to the labs. And that was the easy part.

Afterwards, they would have to exfil overland, through a city of three million dead people, to a tiny airfield on an island out in the lake, for air extraction.

In all the intent activity, Homer, an Alpha operator and former Team Six SEAL, managed to buttonhole Commander Drake – ship's XO and Alpha's liaison and handler on the supercarrier. They now stood together in the shadows of one corner of the mess belowdecks. Homer needed a word in private – specifically, he needed to tell Drake about what he had discovered brewing down in the bowels of the ship. About the dangerous sermon he had overheard in the ship's chapel.

"Yeah, we know about those dudes," Drake said,

as various operators and sailors cruised by in the adjacent passageway, or in one door and out the other. "We call them the Zealots. But you've got to understand – all three of our official chaplains quit those jobs, and took on other duties, after the fall. Well, two of them did. The third we think jumped ship. But, in any case, religion's strictly a volunteer activity these days."

Homer nodded. "I understand, Commander, but you need to be aware this man is preaching some fairly incendiary and seditious stuff. He's saying the Zulus are God's cleaners – and that *we*, the military, are the problem, messing up the End Days and holding up the Rapture."

Drake seemed to take this on board. "Yeah, it's not ideal, is it? But our verdict, when we last discussed it, was that it allowed the men to blow off steam. Nonetheless, I'll make a note to revisit it – send someone down to listen in on Sunday. That square you away, Chief?"

Homer said, "There's something else. I saw a lot of weapons and ordnance piled in a room near the chapel, by the chaplains' quarters."

Someone called Drake's name from the far hatch. He swiveled and made a one-minute sign, then turned back to Homer. "This boat's probably not as shipshape as what you might have been used to. We've got crap stored all over the place these days – hell, we've got a whole organic farm on the hangar deck..." He clapped Homer on the shoulder before heading off. "But I'll make a note to look into that as well. Stand fast, Chief…"

* * *

Four others who had also been in the briefing were Alpha team operators Ali and Pope. Ali was a former Delta sniper – now perhaps the most deadly long gunner left still breathing air; and Pope was a former paramilitary with the CIA Special Activities Division. They were taking fifteen minutes from mission prep and using it to pick the brains of the two British newcomers, Wesley and Martin.

The four of them emerged onto the five-acre flight deck, with its fresh sea air and bit of sun, and headed for the shade of the island. The towering structure, with its blast-proof glass windows and banks and arrays of antennas and dishes, rose up above them into a sky that had been crowding with clouds all afternoon. Either a weather front was coming, or they were sailing into one. The four sat down cross-legged, two with their backs against the steel wall.

"So the Folkestone outbreak was pretty close-run?" Ali asked.

Wesley nodded. "Yes. I remember thinking clearly: *This the end. We're all going to die*. But then the cavalry rolled in."

Martin nodded his agreement. "If an entire mechanized battalion hadn't rocked up when they did,

I have no doubt both of us would be slouching and moaning even now."

Pope looked levelly at the British soldier, and clocked his insignia. "Royal Corps of Engineers."

Martin nodded once. "Fifteen years in. Mostly vehicle maintenance the last couple of years, but a lot of structural prior to that – bases, bridges, great big solid things. I miss all that, come to talk about it…"

Ali looked over at Wesley, still dressed in his UKSS jumpsuit. "What about you. Always been with the Security Services?"

"Yes," nodded Wesley. "Well, I have been since everything went to crap. I worked as a bodyguard before that, and for too many security firms to even remember. Started when I was eighteen, bouncing the doors of a nightclub in a small town in the Midlands. I was actually working in France when it all came down. Caught the last train back to the UK."

"Lucky man," Pope said. "Believe me. We've been back over there many times since."

Wesley looked down at his boots. "Is it as bad as they say?"

Ali nodded solemnly. "And not just France. The whole continent's a dead zone."

"Jesus." Wesley shook his head and squinted off into memory.

"We've moved through a lot of fallen Europe," said Pope. "And you always find the same last stand, played out over and over again – blocked hallways,

14

first-floor stairwells torn down, lot of shotgun shell casings lying around. The odd chef's knife caked with that congealed black shit they have instead of blood. Usually, from the way it's laid out, you can reconstruct the whole battle, their last minutes, blow by blow. It's like a forensic jackpot. If any of that mattered now."

Ali shrugged. "Of course, we turn up far too late to do any good. You can see all this evidence of people desperate for someone to come and save them. But no one ever did. Horror stories that ended with absolute horror. Being devoured – and killed, if they were lucky. Coming back, if they weren't."

Wesley thought of Amarie with a shudder. She had been a woman he had grown close to, during those last weeks of civilization in France. They had only been together a month, but the after-image of that time burned bright in Wesley's mind. The horror that these soldiers had just described – had that been her fate?

Martin grunted. "What a state we've come to – where death is often the best gift you can give someone." He paused while squinting off into his own memory. Then, more quietly, he said, "I had to take off the heads of two of my best young soldiers. With a fire axe from the wall of the hotel."

The Folkestone outbreak had begun when one of the new super-fast zombies, which they called Foxtrot Novembers (for the "fucking nightmare"), had somehow dug its way out of the collapsed Channel

Tunnel – and gotten loose in the barracks where Captain Martin's platoon had been billeted. All had been turned except him.

Pope reached across and put his hand on Martin's shoulder. "Hey. You did what you had to. For everyone's good."

Martin shook his head sadly. "And theirs, too. After the fast one had done the rounds, half of my platoon just laid into the other half, a very nasty fight in very tight quarters. No one made it out of that hotel alive. The upstairs was like some nightmare butcher shop that a tornado had just passed through. The floor was literally a pool of blood and there were bits of people everywhere. They didn't stand a chance. And I knew the best I could do at that point would be to just try and bring the whole building down. I didn't leave with any grenades."

Wesley looked across at his erstwhile partner. "I had to do both of my boys with a shotgun. They were just kids." These were his staff at the security station, who had been out on patrol when the Foxtrot scratched both of them, then disappeared in an eyeblink.

No one replied, but their expressions said it all. *That sucks.*

"With a single-barrel shotgun. I had to stop and reload."

Both Pope and Ali actually thought that was hilarious, and had to carefully swallow their mirth. Pope paused a respectful beat before speaking. "You both did your duty. And next time it might easily be you or me that has to be put down. No one gets a pass."

Ali kept her silence. And as she looked off the edge of the boat, thousands of yards away, toward the horizon, toward the edge of the world, she thought: *What if Homer were turned? Would I have the strength to put him down?* Privately, she doubted she did. She'd turned off hundreds, if not thousands, of living and dead both, in her career as an elite sniper. But this was one shot she could never take.

Would he have the strength to do it for me? she thought, thinking of their semi-secret, and perhaps very ill-advised, love affair. *Oh, God... have we made a terrible mistake — for which we're both going to pay later? Or, much worse, will the whole team pay? Or all of humanity?* A whole world gone down for one misjudged love. It was equally romantic and horrific to contemplate...

Pulling Ali from her reverie, Pope asked the others, "When did you last see the Foxtrot?"

Martin answered. "I saw it go head-first out a window on the top floor of the hotel and hit the ground running. I mean literally running, like it hadn't just fallen twenty feet onto its back. The last time I saw a human move at that kind of speed was when I watched the Olympic 100-meter sprint."

"Word was," Wesley said, "it was also in the battle in the village. But I never saw it. They said it took the concentrated fire of a whole battalion to bring it down."

Martin shook his head. "I don't know what you're all expecting to find in Chicago. But you run into more than a couple of these things at one time… man, you watch your arse."

* * *

Commander Drake appeared from out of a doorway to the island. He strode up to the group, without seeming to have to look around to locate them. (Pope remembered the tracking ship's ID cards that broadcast all their locations.) He addressed one of the newcomers directly.

"Captain Martin. I'm guessing you carry a UK DoD cell phone?"

Mobile, Martin mentally corrected, smiling inwardly at the Americanism. But he just nodded.

"Take a look?" Martin handed it over. "Hmm. High-grade encryption capability. This should connect seamlessly to the ship's packet data network." He began tapping. "Here are guest credentials to get you on… And here's my number." He handed it back. "You think of anything else relevant to this mission, you call me."

Martin almost said, "Aye aye, sir." But instead he just nodded once more.

Drake stalked off again – long, purposeful strides, like he had promises to keep. And nautical miles to go before he'd sleep.

HELLFIRE

Colonel Bryan (or "Doc" Bryan as the men almost always called him), flipped another page of *Coriolanus*. Though the grain riots and the assault on Rome in the story seemed eerily timely, his attention was even less on the book than before. Sitting in a bedside chair in an otherwise empty wardroom of the hospital, he put his bare hand on the grievously wounded operator's forehead again. The digital thermometer would have the last word on his temperature. But Bryan still felt like he could learn more through the touch of bare human skin.

Just so long as it actually remained human.

So far so good. The man was running a moderate fever – but that could be the result of any number of types of infection carried in by the deformed bullet and the gunk upon it. Infection in gunshot wounds was too common, ubiquitous really, even to remark upon. The unconscious operator had been put on massive doses of intravenous antibiotics, plus anti-virals. Aside from that, Bryan had been able to sew his severed neck artery back together, thus usefully keeping the blood in his body. So the patient actually stood a decent chance of surviving.

But, on this occasion, Bryan was a hell of a lot more concerned that if he died, he died properly, and completely. The man was held down with leather wrist and ankle restraints attached to the bed, but nonetheless… Bryan briefly opened one of the man's eyes to check color, dilation, and opacity. Leaning back again, he monitored the man's shallow breathing over the book in his lap. And he exhaled heavily himself.

This burden was his.

* * *

Back out on the helipad, the Black Hawk DAP ("Direct Action Penetrator") that had brought the casualty in was more than a little dinged up itself. The DAP version of the venerable Black Hawk had stub wings mounted with a 30mm automatic cannon, rocket pods, and various other armaments. It had been feared this firepower was going to be needed for the extraction of Echo team. In the event, the bird's pilots had been forced to land amongst a great deal of street debris in order to evacuate the badly wounded operator – during which one of its rocket hardpoints had been damaged by the edge of an overturned car. Two techs from the Aviation Maintenance Company wrestled with it now, trying to unmount an AGM-114 Hellfire laser-guided missile from the dodgy mount.

The two grimy and jumpsuited engineers hunched over the hardpoint, one supporting the missile from below, while the other used his full strength to try and pry it off. Between that, and all the dust in the air from the bird's recent landing, neither noticed the smoke floating out from the base of the stub wing – nor the sparking that was happening underneath the cowling.

There was no getting around that maintenance standards had taken a beating in the ZA – otherwise known as the post-industrial era. The maintenance guys managed to keep the birds flying. But, in this case, the lack of replacement and spare parts meant that the electricals feeding the weapons mounts were long past their expiration date. And the stress of the collision with the car pushed them into overload.

Due to the shorting electricals, one of the Hellfire missiles, which one of the techs still cradled in his arms, ignited. And then it launched.

The aptly named Hellfire, a 106-pound air-to-surface missile, has a shape-charged warhead which packs a 5-million-pound per square inch impact, defeating *all known armor* (back when the enemy could operate things like tanks). Now, as it sparked off, its burning propellant generated 500 foot-pounds of forward force, violently ripping it free of its hardpoint. Normally laser- or radar-guided, the blind and dumb missile simply plowed straight ahead – and directly into the enlisted mess on the opposite side of the compound. Its payload, a high-explosive shape-charged warhead, exploded a fraction of a second after entry, completely destroying most of the building.

And most of the people inside it.

Doc Bryan not only heard, but felt the explosion from where he sat in the hospital. It actually bounced him in his chair. His phone went off a few seconds later.

"Go for Bryan. *What...?* How many?" He listened gravely. "Understood. I can be there in thirty seconds. But I need an orderly here." He looked up from his phone and around the empty wardroom. "Orderly!" he shouted. "Nurse! Anyone!" A panicked-looking young woman in uniform ducked into the room.

"Sir?" she said, fear in her eyes. She already knew something terrible was happening.

"Watch this patient," he said. "Ring me any anomalies. *You do not leave this post.*" He didn't have time to brief her further. "Understand?" She nodded vigorously, but Doc Bryan was already leaping away down the aisle, and out of the room.

OVERRUN

Doc Bryan inserted a morphine syrette into the screaming, badly burnt man lying on the ground before him. He had to get him sedated to work on him – or even to assess him. All the thrashing and flopping around was a danger, to the man himself and to others nearby.

Bryan had set up a triage point 100 meters from the scene where the mess hall had been turned into a flaming inferno by the errant Hellfire. He had to balance precious minutes spent moving critically wounded people around, against the risk of secondary explosions or other hazards close to the blast site. For the better part of twenty minutes now he'd been doing emergency trauma care – most of which consisted of controlling hemorrhaging and airway management – and sending them off on litters to the hospital.

He was so engrossed in care and triage that he'd failed to notice his stretcher bearers had stopped returning to pick up more. He finished fixing a burn mask to the man before him, mentally pronounced him stable, and called out for a litter.

None came.

For the first time in several minutes, Bryan looked and listened attentively around him.

Engrossed in life-or-death tasks, he'd nearly totally zoned out – hadn't even noticed the sounds or tumult of those fighting the fire, and others clearing rubble to pull out survivors. Now, his vision expanding, and his hearing dialing back up, he caught wind of more – and much worse.

Over and above the screams and moans of the wounded nearby, he could make out shrieks from further away. That – and now the sound of gunfire, ramping up fast.

It was all coming from the direction of the hospital.

Doc Bryan squinted off in that direction as a terrible chill seized his heart.

* * *

The Colonel was himself personally pulling hunks of smoking rubble off a crumpled ragdoll of a soldier, around on the opposite side of the destroyed mess, when an MP hailed him, coming up at a gallop – with his sidearm in hand. The Colonel paused and looked up.

"What now, Sergeant?"

The man looked for a second like he didn't know how to answer. Finally he bit the bullet. "Some kind of outbreak, Colonel. Zulus in the hospital. It's complete bedlam, but I'm sure of it. I put one down myself."

"*Jesus fucking…* How many?"

The MP just shook his head, looking like he was fighting down panic.

And then the attack warning signal, a wavering tone across the base-wide speaker system, suddenly rent the air. The Colonel had never heard it – almost no one serving there had. It warbled up and down, chilling the blood of the already half-panicked garrison.

The Colonel dropped his hunk of rock where he stood, and drew his own sidearm. "Roust your entire command. Get them out there setting up a perimeter."

"It's already being done."

"Take me to it."

But the Colonel was already racing off ahead. He knew the way to the hospital.

* * *

Doc Bryan had to fight his way to the hospital himself. It seemed like half the personnel on base were running away from it – and the other half toward. The latter carried rifles, pistols, swords, and in a few cases improvised melee weapons such as shovels. Nearing the main entrance, shoving and being shoved, Bryan pulled up short.

There were four or five bodies lying motionless in a jumble outside the double swinging doors out front. All appeared to be dead of head wounds. From the pallor of their skin... well, Bryan didn't think these people had been alive when they were killed.

He heard someone shout his name from behind. It was one of his young staff doctors – shouting at him to come back, to stay the hell out of there. Fear and guilt raged around in Bryan's breast, battling for control of his body and emotions, and he felt an involuntary sob rise up through his chest. He tried to master himself to take some action, to turn away – but then he looked again at the uniform and hair on one of the bodies. This one faced away from him, but was still bracingly familiar.

Gripped with horror, afraid to continue or to stop, he squatted down, leaned over... and rolled the body over. He couldn't recognize the face. Much of it, in particular the nose, looked like it had been bitten off. Also, the base of her skull was a large gaping wound, from a gunshot, or shotgun blast. But her name patch on her blouse was intact. It was the nurse he had called in to watch the wounded Echo operator, when he ran off to the scene of the disaster at the mess hall.

He found he could now see, so clearly, reconstructed in his mind's eye, though largely against his will, the nurse leaning over the patient, perhaps in response to him stirring, or convulsing... leaning over him close enough for him, or rather it, to snap its head upward, to stretch its neck out... and to bite. It must have gnawed through much of her face before she managed to pull away.

And then there would have been two zombies in

the hospital. And only one of them tied down.

Unseen hands grasped Bryan by the arms and pulled him away.

On either side, flowing around him, four or five operators with assault rifles to their shoulders poured inside the hospital through the double doors.

* * *

"Sitrep!" the Colonel shouted, though not to anyone in particular. He was now the ranking officer on the scene. But, so far, no one really seemed to be running this battle.

An operator the Colonel recognized from Charlie team pulled his eye from his rifle sight and spoke in that inimitable ice-cool drawl of SOF guys in a crisis: "We've got something like a perimeter, Colonel. Could stand to firm it up, but I don't think anything's getting out. We've been putting down squirters as they appear." He snapped his sight back to his eye as a shadowed figure lurched past an upper-story window. But it was gone just as quickly. "On the other hand… I've seen a couple of groups of guys go in." He paused to spit on the ground, toward the building. "Haven't seen anyone come out."

The Colonel nodded and took a beat to process all of that. "Okay, spread the word. *No one* else goes inside. You hold here until relieved. Got it?"

"Roger that."

The Colonel took a few precious seconds to

survey the shifting lines of the skirmish. He considered touring the perimeter around to the other side. But there was little point, and less time. He turned on his heel and headed for the helo hangars.

At a flat run.

* * *

Captain Charlotte Maidstone, British Army Air Corps, and ranking Apache pilot and gunner, jumped off the couch in the pilots' ready room when the door crashed open and banged against the wall. The rules for on-call combat pilots were clear: the world could be coming down in great sheets of shit, and she'd still have stay right where she was in the ready room. So there she'd sat, first hearing the earth-shaking explosion, then the shouting – then the firing and the wailing siren. No one had told her anything. Hardly anyone had answered when she tried to ask. She'd just had to sit there and listen to it.

Now, seeing the Colonel himself blast in behind the rocketing door, she could reasonably hope the moment had come to get her guns into the fight. Whatever the fight was.

"You fly that dragon?" the Colonel asked, jabbing his thumb over his shoulder at the nearest Apache parked up in the hangar.

"Affirmative."

"It armed and fueled?"

"Tanks topped – and Hellfires, rockets, and

thirty mil topped off, too."

"You're on me," he said. "Get us airborne."

As they ran to the hangar, he asked about the rockets.

"Hydra 2.75-inch," she said. "Flechette loads."

As Captain Maidstone ran up the APC and began bringing the bird to life, the Colonel climbed into the front seat. When she climbed into the rear, pulling her full-face helmet on, he said to her, "I have full authority for what happens now. You understand me?"

She didn't understand, but she nodded her assent and got them taxiing out of the hangar. Fourteen minutes after the Colonel walked in her door, she had them rising and banking over the chaos of Hereford. Below them, they could see smoke rising from several points.

And bodies running everywhere.

* * *

Doc Bryan struggled to master himself now, as the chaos finally subsided all around them. The outbreak was over.

Though, how they were going to deal with this many casualties was beyond him – never mind without the hospital. He had to struggle mightily to control his emotions – to stay effective and do his job in the midst of all this. The sounds of the most recent explosions, and the whizzing of zipping metal, still echoed in his ears.

One of the operators, smeared with soot and blood, holding his rifle low, was patiently explaining to him what had just happened.

"Flechette loads, Doc – 96 darts per warhead. The Colonel fired a spread of flechette rockets down the entire length of the hospital. I can guarantee you anything in there with a head had it skewered with a sharp sliver of metal. But a lot of people holding the perimeter were hit, too. I've got several guys with big-ish holes in 'em. Know you won't mind patching 'em up…"

Bryan shook his head to try and clear it. The hospital was of course a no-go zone, for the duration. The enlisted mess was out, as it had just been destroyed. The motor pool garage was probably the next biggest structure. He'd start setting up an ad hoc medical facility in there. There would be med supplies in various places – in vehicles, in aircraft, in medics' rucks. And he'd start medevac'ing everyone he could out to Bristol, Birmingham, or London… civilian hospitals, wherever could take them… He had a million things to do now, and lives hung on the balance of every decision.

But at least the living would live, or many of them; and the dead would stay dead.

For now.

* * *

The Colonel slumped behind his desk, the adrenaline finally draining out of him. He was on the horn to CentCom. Shit was very far from under control. But at least there was enough structure around him, a lot of ongoing crisis management, that he could pretend to be a commander again. And not some goddamned half-assed aerial rocketeer.

"It wasn't just a matter of saving the base, General," he said tiredly into the phone. "I put to you that this base is also the last best hope for humanity. As goes Hereford, so goes the world. Saving this facility was worth any price short of destroying it." He listened and nodded for a few seconds more. "Yes, I was up in the helo myself. And, yes, I directed the rocket fire into the center of the outbreak… Copy that, sir. Yes, you'll get my full report." He hung up the phone.

And he waved in the half dozen people at the door who needed something from him. Outside, the sun was going down; but the real work was just beginning.

In his last second before the chaos of command washed over him again, he thought:

This goddamned job was more fun before all the fucking zombies.

Making terrible decisions that cost men their lives never got any easier. But it seemed to be getting a whole lot more necessary lately…

LAUNCH

Several able seamen and a couple of flight deck ratings, plus the small aircrew, pitched in to help load up the plane that sat waiting on the flight deck. But Alpha team did most of the loading themselves.

This wasn't because they were overly precious about how their gear was handled. They were just accustomed to rolling up their sleeves and doing whatever needed doing. That they could make a headshot from a mile out, parachute into combat from 40,000 feet wearing SCUBA gear, speak Farsi, and hack computer networks didn't mean that they were too good to carry their own shit.

"Get it done," was one of the most commonly heard phrases in their world, the SOF world. Most often as in, "Right. We'll get it done."

Pallets of gear, ammo boxes, weapons, explosives, radios, parachute rigs, and crates and rucks of God knows what else got carried, rolled, heaved, and power-lifted into the rear half of the C-2A Greyhound. Its top-mounted wings, each with an underslung propeller engine, loomed over the ducking heads of the men. The flight deck was starkly lit with LED and sodium lights in the black middle of the night, shadows looming in every corner, all of it out in the inky blackness of the rolling Atlantic. Ordinarily, pre-Apocalypse, they would have been able to spot the lights of Norfolk and Virginia Beach off in the distance on the coast – at the edge of a mighty continent.

Now, of course, it was all black.

Heavy cloud cover also masked the stars and moon above. The wind foretold of a storm coming. The whole eastern half of the United States seemed to be socked in. But it was no good waiting for better weather – even if an accurate forecast could be produced. There was truly no time like the present. Especially when the present may be all you've got.

Two people who did not load shit were Commander Drake and Master Gunnery Sergeant Fick, the commander of the Marine Special Operations team onboard – who were also the B team and QRF (Quick Reaction Force) in case Alpha got in trouble. They stood with their bare arms folded, in a windy open area between the hulking island and the base of Catapult #3, the one at the starboard waist – or, rather, the Electromagnetic Aircraft Launch System (EMALS) that had replaced the traditional steam catapults. When kicked off, it would accelerate the 59,000-pound fully loaded aircraft from 0 to 160mph in two seconds.

As the loading finished up, and final flight checks were made… and as the seven men and one woman of Alpha team slung themselves coolly and emotionlessly into the front passenger section of the cabin… Captain Ainsley, formerly of SAS Increment, and commander of the team, stepped aside, and strode up to Drake and Fick, for a last word. Both the naval officer and the Marine senior NCO instinctively saluted. An habitual gesture, made for those going into harm's way, by those who have been there.

"Right. Thanks for the hospitality," Ainsley said with a serious look, saluting back.

"It's been our pleasure," Drake responded. "More where it came from, when you get back."

Ainsley's expression softened slightly at that, almost a smile, as if the idea of them coming back was funny. Then it faded. "You'll ring us immediately you hear from Hereford?"

"Absolutely, Captain," Drake said.

Ainsley reached out to shake his hand. "Just buggered comms again, no doubt."

Drake nodded, taking his hand.

Fick put out his. "We'll be on a short tether here. You fly safe." Ainsley raised his eyebrow but shook the Marine's hand, then turned on his heel and marched off again.

Fick looked across to Drake. "They can't reach Hereford?"

"Couldn't," Drake said. "Actually, we just got through ten minutes ago."

The pair were both having to yell now over the roar of the plane's prop engines, which were revving up to full power. The holdback bar at its rear held the trembling aircraft in place, while green-shirted flight deck crew attached the towbar to the plane's nose.

"And?" Fick shouted.

"It was an outbreak. Bad. They lost nearly 20% of their total strength – dead, wounded, or turned. Their colonel had to get in an Apache and rocket their own goddamned hospital."

"Jesus Christ's nuts on a hotplate. You're not gonna tell Alpha?"

"Negative," Drake said, shaking his head slowly. "There's not a blessed thing they can do about it from here. And the last thing these guys need is one more damned thing to worry about." He crossed his arms and squinted into the dazzling lights. "On top of saving the world."

With that, the catapult officer (or "shooter") did his final checks from the control pod, approved the pressure, and fired the release. The holdback bar dropped, the towbar yanked forward remorselessly – and the plane, and everyone packed into it, shrieked down half the length of the flight deck like, well, something shot out of a catapult. The bird dropped off the edge of the deck, briefly disappeared from sight, then reappeared, whining as it gained altitude.

And then its landing lights all went dark. After that, there was only a fading buzzing sound, heading for the greater darkness of land – for the very middle of the land of the dead.

And perhaps the last hope for the living.

FLIGHT

"Hey, wait a minute," growled Predator, the team's enormous and unkillable assaulter, in that voice that always reminded Ali of a professional wrestler doing a beef jerky commercial. "I saw exactly one of these cargo planes. So how do the Marines come bail our asses out if this one gets taken down…?"

Command Sergeant Major Handon, former Delta shooter, team's ranking NCO, and 2IC to Captain Ainsley, leaned back in the darkness of the cabin. Aside from a couple of low-level red combat lights, the plane was totally blacked out. He knitted his fingers together behind his head. For some reason, he was never so relaxed as in the hours and minutes before a combat jump, or combat insertion by helo. Any kind of flying leap into probable death and destruction seemed to soothe his nerves.

"Sea Hawks," he said, referring to the Navy UH-60-variant helos that lived on the deck of the destroyer, the USS *Michael Murphy*, which had sailed along with the *Kennedy*. "Big fuel bladders inside… and a one-way trip. It was all in the MARSOC briefing."

"What the hell kind of a rescue is that? *One way?*"

Pope looked up from a paperback volume of Dostoevsky he'd scored from the carrier's library, around which he was curled in a dark corner of the cramped cabin. "Escape and evade, big guy. It all goes south, we presume you'll hijack a monster car-crushing truck and drive us all to the coast."

Predator looked mollified. "Okay. That could work."

Juice, the team's signals and tech genius, bearded and puffy, formerly of the secretive spec-ops intelligence unit known as "The Activity," looked thoughtful. "I guess Mexico's out. Heh. Should have listened to the damned Republicans and locked down the border when we still had a chance to…"

Pope went back to his book.

Handon closed his eyes and dozed off.

* * *

Homer and Ali sat face to face in the row behind.

At this point, they both pretty much knew everyone else knew about the two of them. Somehow they didn't feel like going through any more contortions to conceal it. Maybe it was that their chances of survival had gone from slim, in their normal duties, to none, on this mission. And if they did somehow survive, well, everyone could just go on pretending.

Ali figured that even if they achieved their target and found the data on the vaccine, which seemed just about doable… well, after that, fighting their way through downtown Chicago to their extraction point was a *whole* other proposition. Three million Zulus (and Romeos, the runners – and maybe Foxtrots, the insanely lethal ones…) in a blighted and constricted urban space were going to make *Black Hawk Down* and the Battle of Mogadishu look like a sorority house pillow fight.

Ali, for her part, didn't know if it might not be better this way. Her whole life had been about trying to do something useful. And you didn't get to the Tier-1 level in spec-ops if you weren't totally ready to get killed doing it. She knew what Predator would say, about the looming spectre of the team's death, if she were brave enough to raise it with him: "Today's as good a day as any. Let's finish it right." Juice would probably make some noises about being smarter, not braver. But in the end he would stand and fight with Pred, and with all of them. Both Handon and Ainsley, despite their differences, would do their jobs until their last breaths. And probably a few seconds beyond that.

And Homer… well, Homer would be happy enough to go when God said it was his time. She didn't believe that meant anything, of course. Except in that it always gave him a reason to go on, and kept his spirits up even in their worst moments. That was real. She looked up into his eyes, glinting in the darkness. She reached out for his hand.

"Suppose," she said, quietly and carefully, "that you actually do loop through your whole life in the last second before you die. That it all flashes by. And then you wink out. How different is that, really, from looping through that one second over and over for eternity?"

Homer nodded and took this in. "Are you saying the soulless are replaying their lives over and over?" He thought immediately of Job, his Existential Zulu, standing forlorn on his Dover clifftop. Standing guard by his friend.

Ali shook her head slightly. "I don't know. I always feel like I can see something in there. Behind their eyes."

Homer squeezed her hand. "Sister… just don't you ever find out."

She realized with embarrassment that a tear was forming at the corner of her eye. Homer had his God for comfort. And she had Homer.

And for that she would always be profoundly grateful.

* * *

For his part, Homer did not want to look away from her. But he did, out the window, and down, toward the endless continent that now loomed beneath them. He was also looking to the north. Little Creek, Virginia would be out there, maybe only 75 or 100 miles distant.

Which meant that his family would also be down there, somewhere. In some state, his family would be there.

When the reality of that fact hit home, it was all he could do not to grab his parachute rig, pop the door, and dive. To be so close, and to not know, to do nothing... all of it was insane.

Part of him also wanted to pull his hand away from Ali's.

Instead, he tightened his grip.

Wherever his wife and daughter and son were... they would be clinging to whatever they had left. Whether it was each other, or to the bosom of the Almighty.

If it pleases God to let me pass through this one last storm, he thought... *I swear on my immortal soul that I will go and find them. One way or another, whatever the outcome... I will go to them.*

* * *

Henno, the other Brit and SAS veteran, and a fierce Yorkshireman, slept through almost the whole flight. Operators spend a lot of time on long-haul aircraft, and have a well-honed ability to rack out quickly, anywhere. But Henno had taken kipping to an art form. It was his favorite pastime.

He came awake calmly and completely when the red cabin lights flashed the 15-minute warning. He yawned, grabbed his gear and rifle, and smiled out loud.

He'd been dreaming of a big fry-up, sausage and mushrooms and beans on toast, in his native North

Yorkshire. He wondered if he'd ever see the beautiful North York Moors again.

Yeah, no danger, he thought. He always thought that way. With a childlike faith.

Ainsley clapped him on the shoulder, as they all stood and began to get rigged up for the jump. This included switching over to their oxygen bottles, and checking one another for signs of hypoxia. Also, every rig and connection needed to be triple-checked. The plane tilted and the engines screamed as the pilot coaxed it to its service ceiling of 33,500 feet.

The ammo cache pallet got shoved out the door first, into the screaming wind and rain.

After that, everything moved very, very quickly.

ON THE AIR

Thousands of miles back to the east, Alice Grisham nodded at the cameraman and then at the bedraggled man standing next to her, then raised the microphone. The wind was blasting across the field as her hair flailed around her, and she wished she had tied it back that morning. But they had been in a hurry. As one of only three television news crews still functioning, they had to move fast to get a drop on anything new, to get there before it was all over. And getting down to Folkestone as soon as possible that morning had been more important than good grooming.

"Are we on air?" she said, trying to focus on the wavering camera.

"Yes, we're go."

"Hello and welcome to Midland Central News. This morning I'm in Folkestone, where the most astounding story has been uncovered overnight. I'm here with Mr. Alderney, who is originally from Paris, but until recently has been a resident of none other than the Channel Tunnel. For the last two years, nearly forty people have been fighting for their lives inside the tunnel itself, and in the early hours of this morning troops from the barracks here in Folkestone initiated an astounding operation to clear out a zombie infestation threatening to break out of the tunnel and onto our streets. But what they were to discover inside was far more profound than zombies. No fewer than thirty-eight survivors have so far been recovered, including a young child who was in fact born inside. Mr. Alderney, how does it feel to be out of the tunnel?"

The man coughed, and stuttered before managing to speak.

"It's. Unspeakable. My English is not so good. I am not able to say how this feels. To be free and out from this place now."

"That's wonderful, Mr Alderney. Please, if you don't mind, we haven't been able to speak to the mother of the child, but could you tell us anything about her?"

"Oh the girl, she is so beautiful, she is what keep us all going all this time. Little Josie and her mother Amarie have been our driving to be free. So pretty she is and a lifeline to us all. I am sorry; my eyes are hurting from the light."

"And am I correct that she was born inside the tunnel, whilst you were trapped down there?"

"Yes. Yes. She was born in the back of a car in the maintenance tunnel. We had not doctor or nurse, but we had a... *paramèdical* with us. We thought that they would both die, because it was not a good birth, but they made it through."

"That is an amazing story. Please tell us what it was like to live in the tunnel. Were there many zombies down there?"

"Oh, God. Many of them. We had to fight with metal bars to keep them away. We lost some people as well. Those were the worst to have to kill. Then we managed to make a... *barrière?*... of the wreckage to keep them away from the supply train but still some manage to get over it. We were living in the maintenance tunnel. No zombies there and we had to always keep the doors shut."

"And you lived in the dark all this time, with only the food from the supply train?"

"Yes. But not all in the dark. One of the other men, he is an electrician from the train company and he find electrical points that are not switched off. We are able to make lighting in some places. Yes, we survived on the food from the supply train."

"I would imagine you are looking forward to eating and sleeping somewhere other than in the tunnel today?"

"Oh yes. So much. I don't mind what. Anything but tuna."

The cameraman panned the camera thirty degrees, focusing beyond the reporter, to the road. A soldier was pointing at the camera and barking orders to those around him.

Alice noticed this, glanced over her shoulder, saw the soldiers approaching, and then turned back to the camera.

"Thank you all for tuning in, we will try to report

more news as we uncover it. Alice Grisham reporting for Midland Central News live from Folkestone, where survivors from the Channel Tunnel have this morning been rescued, including a small child born in the tunnel itself."

TO THOSE WHO WAIT

The bowels of the *JFK* were like an endless maze, with countless passageways and compartments spreading out across multiple decks. Two years ago, before the fall, the ship had been home to nearly 5,000 crew, and all of that space had been occupied and in use almost every day. But as the number of crew dwindled, more and more compartments on the lower decks became abandoned and disused. Many of these stored scavenged goods that the expedition teams had thought might be of use at some point, but much of it had proven unnecessary, and slowly but surely many of the areas were left closed, unlit, and untended.

In the very early days of the plague, even the ship's executive officer, Drake, hadn't realized the full extent of the risk – until it became apparent that just stepping on shore was dangerous, let alone failing to meticulously check those who came back.

That was how Brian Marlin had got back on board, days before they introduced the quarantine procedure of holding expedition members on the support ship. That was how, after the small skirmish that had left two of his team dead, Brian had returned to his duties, with no one even noticing the small scratch below his left ear that the undead creature had managed to inflict on him just as he smashed its head onto the pavement and crushed it with a trash can. Hell, Brian hadn't even noticed the scratch at the time, and when he saw it later, while shaving and trying to forget about the half dozen or so creatures that they had fought, he just shrugged it off and figured that he had caught himself on the furniture in the bar, or perhaps the dumpster in the alley.

He had been drunk after all; they all had. When the fight had broken out he had thought, like all of them, that their assailants were either also drunk or were street bums desperate to take advantage of a group of drunken sailors on their way back to ship after an evening of shore leave. They'd jumped them in the alleyway, appearing out of the dark before any of the seamen had a chance to clock them. Before he or any of his fellows could react, two of the group had been pulled to the ground, and blood splashed everywhere.

Of course, he hadn't just scratched himself on the rusty dumpster. From the moment that the zombie's finger, with its sharp and broken bone poking out of torn, dead flesh, had pierced his skin, causing a thin, half-inch-long line of blood to well up and dry quickly, Brian Marlin's fate had already been foreclosed.

The sickness had come quickly. He'd woken up and rushed to the toilet, hurling his guts up. *Oh God, too much beer*, he had thought – but then he had seen the color of the water in the bottom of the pan. It wasn't brown, or yellow, or just some mixture of his dinner the night before and eight large glasses of draught beer. No. The bottom of the toilet pan was splattered with black and red.

He'd flushed the toilet and walked away, telling himself it was just the wings turning a strange color with the beer, and stumbled out into the passageway. *I'll walk for a bit*, he thought, *maybe go up on deck and get some air and clear my head*. But that hadn't worked. He'd stood up on the flight deck and breathed in the night air and felt even worse.

An hour later and Brian Marlin was sitting in the storeroom two decks below his own berth, in the place where he and his shipmates would sometimes play cards and lose a few dollars here and there, out of the way where no one could see. He rocked backward and forward hoping that the sickness would pass. It had been the only place that he could think of at the time to sit quietly and not be disturbed; not be ridiculed by his fellows for not holding his drink. He hadn't locked the door, just in case he passed out and needed help.

His head swam and his stomach churned over and over, and he found himself focusing on the labels of the boxes that were stacked along one of the walls – 5.56mm rounds, many thousands of them.

Only his own team noticed him missing, but none of them had time to report it since the next morning they were back on shore, ordered to attempt to quell the rioting in the city. Not a single one of them returned.

Of course it had turned out not to be a riot at all, and the following morning, while Commander Drake was busy trying to put together all of the new information that was coming from all directions, and attempting to restore some kind of order to the shocked carrier strike group, Brian Marlin passed out in the darkness of storeroom 34 and never woke up again.

At least not alive.

Of course, it was not likely that a zombie could have stayed hidden and unnoticed on its own, on a warship, for two years, even locked away in a room on the lower decks that was rarely visited. It was Aaron Carson, a man who in the last year or so had started being called by another name – the Preacher – that found Marlin, or what was left of him.

Carson was young, and had only been on the ship for six months of his first tour when he found the creature in the disused storeroom. He was still in his apprenticeship, and at the time still thinking he was lucky as hell to be onboard the *JFK* so early in his career. The carrier was the goddess of the seas, the most powerful ship ever to sail, and he was one of the people responsible for making sure she was solid. He was a steelworker by trade and – until the reports of attacks in the city during shore leave came floating back – he had been content. He kept to himself, not paying much attention to the rest of the world or to the news. His strict religious upbringing had carved him into a quiet introvert.

Weeks after the quarantine procedure was put in place, he'd gone down to the lower decks, the storage areas, searching for fuel cells for a blowtorch. It had taken him six compartments before he found one in the locker of storeroom 34. The locker was a massive metal thing, about eight feet tall and six wide, and previously would have been used to safely store larger ordnance such as man-portable missile launchers. But it had been emptied at some point and all that was in it now was a case of fuel cells just like the one he needed. He took out the case, opened it, and began measuring it up when he heard the noise.

Thunk.

He frowned, put down the fuel cell and peered through the room, looking to the entrance. The door was still open, and he heard noises from the corridor, but they were faint; the normal sounds of the ship. This had been closer, definitely in the room with him.

He stood up, took a few steps forward and peered around the corner. The room was an L shape, curving around the back of the next storage area. He saw stacks of boxes, ammunition by the looks of them, but it was darker around there; the light must have been out.

"Who's there?" he asked, instinctively lowering his hand to his waist. Silly of him – only MPs and a few officers carried sidearms while onboard ship.

Thunk. The sound again. What the hell was that? He stepped around the corner, peering into the darkness.

"Is anybody in there?"

No answer. Maybe it had been a rat.

Then something moved in the darkness much closer to him. He felt his chest lurch as a shadow passed behind the stack of crates closest to him.

Carson grabbed for the nearest thing he had to a weapon – the blowtorch he'd laid down before him. He was too slow, and he knew it. He meant to call out, but whatever it was stumbled from behind the stack of crates and lunged toward him. He spun sideways, swinging the blowtorch, and managed to dodge a clumsy attack, smacking the unknown assailant around the side of the face. The creature's cheek burst open with a crunch, splashing black gunk across the floor, and then it fell forward into the locker.

Carson was faster this time, and stepped forward, pushing the zombie hard so that its whole body fell into the bottom of the locker. It tried to fight back, reaching for him, and managed to snatch the cuff of his shirt. But Carson panicked and flailed and its grip loosened, just for a moment. It was enough for him to grab the open locker door and slam it shut.

He fell to the floor, breathing heavily, nearly retching at the stink that now assaulted his nostrils. It was too much. He emptied the contents of his stomach onto the floor.

As Carson sat there, trying to recover from the shock of seeing an actual zombie on the carrier, he heard a dull thud from inside the locker, then another. It was very quiet. Those lockers had thick walls and the thing that he had trapped inside was apparently very weak.

What the hell would he do now? Would he tell his commanding officer? He had to, didn't he? Or did he? If the chain of command found out that there was a zombie on board, the ship would become chaos as they quarantined everything and everyone nearby, anyone who might have come into contact. That included him. *Oh God, no.* Quarantine drove him nuts. He couldn't do that again. He would just leave it in there for a while, while he decided how best to deal with it.

That had been nearly two years ago.

Carson had kept it all to himself, in the end. The creature in the locker. God's cleaner. After a week it had already been too late to tell anyone, he belatedly realized – he'd have been court-martialed, if not lynched. Anyone who opened the locker would have been able to figure out that the thing had been in there longer than a few minutes; they would have discovered it and that would have been the end of him. It would have meant exile – out into the blossoming ZA.

Of course, once he opened the locker and tied the thing up – a task that had proven nearly as dangerous as the first encounter – it had been more or less safe. Once it was bound and gagged with thick layers of duct tape it could barely move. The bumping against the side of the locker stopped. People rarely went down to storeroom 34 unless they wanted 5.56 ammunition, and he moved some of that to a room nearer the section entrance. He'd used the locker key to lock it up, and kept it with him, around his neck on a chain, so that no one else would be able to open it and discover what he had done.

After a few weeks, his curiosity started to itch. What could he find out from the fell creature? How had God allowed such a thing to exist? Could he discover something from that rotting, undead but walking corpse that no one else had been able to fathom?

Over the months that followed he examined the zombie repeatedly, marvelling at how a creature with no living organs could still be alive. All things are equal in the eyes of God, are they not? Surely this thing must be a creation of the Almighty? Surely its presence here was some kind of miracle? As the weeks passed, Carson began to spend more and more of his time off duty sitting facing his captive. There were answers in those eyes, he was sure of it.

Slowly, but inevitably, Aaron Carson's mind began to twist. His sanity ebbed as the days passed. He was still able to do his job, but more and more he went to the chapel, to where the chaplain would give his sermons, so he could listen. He asked questions about zombies, pushed and prodded the chaplain, whose faith was already waning, with constant theories that made the man peer at him like he was some sort of leech.

How dare he look at me like that? Carson had cursed, and he became convinced that the chaplain was not worthy of his position. The man was blatantly gutless and weak, and the idea that he could preach the word of God an insult.

When the chaplain didn't turn up to mass one day, people talked. There was a search, but they never found him, and the last time he had been seen by anyone – at least, anyone who would speak up – he had been spotted heading for the fantail deck late at night. A lot of people knew that was where he spent some of his off-duty time, quietly and in prayer. It was presumed that the man, who had recently shown many signs of stress and strain, had simply jumped from the ship, into the cold waves of the Pacific. And in a way they would have been right. The chaplain was indeed floating in the waves many miles away and just below the surface.

But he hadn't gone there voluntarily.

Without a Christian chaplain to lead prayer, meetings had been reduced to quiet contemplation for most. There was no one to speak the word of God, or no one willing to take up the book and attempt to guide folks. Until one evening, when there was a particularly low attendance, Carson stood up, walked to the front, picked up the Bible from the small table, opened it and began to speak. He didn't speak from the book itself, instead feeling that he was driven by God himself to speak his own words, channeling the thoughts of the Almighty, the thoughts given to him when sitting staring into the eyes of his undead guest in the locker of storeroom 34.

"In the End Days, when the Rapture was upon the Earth, the last remaining pure souls would be called upon to fight one last battle, one great battle against the most evil of enemies…"

And people had listened. Two years had passed since the Apocalypse began, months of prayer and preaching to his followers, those amongst the crew that felt their world was lost. But he had changed all that. He, Aaron Carson, now the Preacher, was a guide to the lost. Slowly his audience had grown, and so had those that he could trust. Those who also believed that they should welcome the will of God, that they should return to their homeland, return to their homes and die, and then ascend, as they were intended to.

From a few, to a few dozen. Then more, many more. By the time the carrier left on its journey back to the USA, its first such homecoming in six months, his following numbered nearly a hundred. On the night when the special forces from the UK flew off, over *his* native soil, his country, a place where they didn't belong, Aaron Carson decided that it was time to go home.

"This day, my brothers and sisters, we watched as the avatars of evil flew into our homeland for some secret purpose that we are not privy to. What are they looking for, I wonder? To steal what should rightfully be ours? A gift from God to those who are faithful, guarded by millions of his followers?"

A murmur went through the assembled crowd, and nods of agreement.

"You all noticed, did you not, how they even sent one of their own amongst us? A spy sent into our ranks, like they thought that they could fool us. That we are stupid?" He meant Homer – who had come down simply to pray, but had become alarmed and taken a probing look around the compartments of the Zealots.

Louder murmurs and angry faces looked back at Carson.

"But we are not stupid. We are not fools. And so long as they believe that we are, we have the advantage of surprise. We are, for the first time in many months, merely yards from our home shore. Our homeland. It is time that we make a stand and take what is rightfully ours. In the name of God. And this is how we are going to do it…"

ZEALOTRY UNLEASHED

Now Carson stood once again in storeroom 34, looking at the locker, while next to him were two of his henchmen. He had never called them that, but these were his most trusted followers. Right now, others would be moving into place, and in less than fifteen minutes their uprising would begin. All on cue, and all according to schedule, his followers would take up key positions, by deadly force where necessary. The ship's nuclear reactors, the weapons caches, and the bridge. With many of the officers and sailors in the island busy with preparations for the plane's return and its refueling, few would be watching the other areas of the ship, and certainly not the movements of a hundred or so of Carson's faithful.

"Do not be fearful, my brothers," he said as he opened the locker and revealed the zombie. Neither of the other two moved; both looked at the creature with mild alarm. They had not run, as he been worried they might.

"This, my brothers, is where I have gained all of my answers. Fools may believe that these are monstrous creatures, but as we know they cannot be. For were they not originally made in God's likeness?

Did he not create each one of them? This change has been his will, and by long study and contemplation, God has told me his will. Now we shall release this creature and guide it toward our enemies."

They hauled the zombie out of the locker and stood it up. The stench was overpowering, but neither of the men showed any signs of weakness.

Carson stood facing it, reached forward and pulled off some of the duct tape that had kept it incapacitated all these months, just from its legs for now. Then they began to walk it ahead of them through the dim passageways. Around them, the hum of the ship, the background noise that was always there, disguised the low groaning that the zombie now made. The henchmen held one arm each, with Carson guiding it by a rope tied around its neck. They took it up two flights of stairs, quietly avoiding the few sailors who worked nearby. Carson had carefully checked the duty logs, and knew exactly which berthing compartment to go to. The carrier required staffing 24 hours a day, and that meant people sleeping at all hours.

He peered through the door that was slightly ajar, then turned and nodded. The nearer henchman pushed the zombie forward and began to cut the duct tape that bound it. It started to struggle, to reach for them, but they pushed it into the room as the last of the duct tape gave way. Carson reached forward to pull the strip from the creature's mouth, just as a sailor in one of the nearby bunks began to stir.

What no one was expecting was the speed with which the zombie moved. Carson had always believed the thing to be one of the slow-moving ones. He had no information, and no way to consider that the fast ones, the new nightmares that could spread the virus like lightning, were actually an evolution of the earliest victims. This creature had been dormant for two years, hidden away in the locker. Its body had not deteriorated nearly as much as those that walk the Earth – but its behavior had evolved dramatically.

Carson stepped back out the door as the follower on his left pulled it shut. They would close the door and listen while the creature turned those in the room. It wouldn't matter if people awoke. They would not be quick enough to realize they had the walking dead in their midst.

But that wasn't what happened next.

As the henchman pulled on the door he felt a pain in his wrist. Black and filthy fingernails dug into his arm as the zombie tore into him, shredding the skin and bursting the veins. Blood squirted out as the artery was sliced open, splattering Carson and the other man, blinding them both for long enough to leave them dazed as the zombie rushed back out the door. In a flash, it raked its other hand across the face of the second henchman, at the same time lunging forward and sinking its teeth into Carson's face. All three men lurched backward, shock and fear incapacitating them as the creature bit and clawed. Carson reached for the gun in his waistband, drew it and fired, but he couldn't see clearly, and the round tunneled straight through the chest of the first henchman, who stopped clutching at his wrist and fell to the ground.

And with that, the zombie was gone, rushing back into the room behind it to attack the twenty sailors asleep in the bunks. Carson staggered backward, stopped himself from falling to the floor, and stumbled away down the corridor. He glanced back at his men, unable to speak even a word. At that very moment, the dead henchman began to twitch. Carson ran. He ran all the way to the hospital ward on the floor above, passing several people on the way, but not saying a word. At least one person called out to him, but he didn't stop. He just kept running until he could lock himself away.

He yanked open the door, forgetting to shut it behind him, pulled open a cabinet and came up with a fistful of bandages. The blood from his face was pouring down his neck fast and, as Carson looked into the mirror beside the cabinet, he noticed the skin around the wound – a gaping hole that made him faint to behold – was turning grey and mottled. Small tendrils of dark coloring were already spreading from it. He panicked, grabbing hold of the mirror to steady himself, now revealing claw marks on his arms. More pale skin and spiderweb lines of darkness were appearing, as he watched the virus spread and take hold.

Carson's chest heaved as he struggled to breathe.

The asphyxiation, he thought. The lack of breath. His heart thumping slower and slower. All were signs of the infection, but this was too fast, much faster than he had known it could be.

Aaron Carson slumped down onto the floor and stared at his hands. Around him, the distant sounds of gunfire began to echo through the halls. His followers had begun their mutiny. Soon the ship would be in their hands, but now... now he would not be there to lead them in the way that he had envisioned.

How could this be? he thought. This was not the will of God, not what was promised. This was wrong. He was supposed to lead the chosen few home, not become one of God's cleaners.

THROUGH GLADDEN FIELDS

Corey Westrow prodded the soil and frowned at the wilting potato plant in front of him. He stood up, stretched, and shook his head in disgust at the spreading patch of dying plants. He was completely puzzled by it. Up until the last few days, this hangar had been the ideal place for growing crops – even more so than his father's fields, and that was saying something. Everyone thought of Idaho for potatoes, of course. But Washington state, with its gorgeous soil plus the wet and chilly weather everyone complained about, had the most productive potato fields in the world. Well, used to have.

But now that same soil, dug from the ground not far from the fields his father had tended, and hauled in sacks onboard and then down to the cavernous hangar deck of the *JFK*, had given no fewer than four life-saving crops to the thousands aboard the surviving ships of the strike group. It had taken the work crews a week of going backward and forward to the mainland to gather enough soil and wood to build the farm – a week that Drake had not wanted to spend with the carrier sitting so near to shore. But it had been worth it. Corey looked across the dimly lit deck. He glanced up at the racks of UV lighting that they had installed, all taken from a warehouse on the outskirts of Seattle, and then over the endless rows of crop beds packed with spreading plants.

It had worked a treat so far, but now something was amiss. He guessed that it was the drainage, or the sea air, or maybe the water filtration was failing somehow. His father would have gotten to the bottom of it quickly, no doubt. And Corey wished that his father were here now to berate him for not airing the soil enough, or not turning it over a third or fourth time. It's all in the preparation, that's what his dad had drilled into him from the moment he had grown old enough to walk and watch his father on the farm. As he had approached manhood, though, Corey became convinced that it was a hopeless profession, farming the fields while most of the other Irish immigrant families to the region had long ago taken up work as bankers, merchants, publishers, politicians, mine owners – anything to escape the grip of the single crop that had devastated Ireland. Like them, Corey longed for something else.

In spite of his current troubles, he laughed loudly at how ridiculous it all was, really – imagining the look on his father's face if he had lived to see the world's most powerful warship with its aircraft hangar deck full of potato beds. He laughed bitterly at how he had left his father and that farm on the hillside to run off and join the Navy. The catering corps had been ideal for him, the escape that he had needed and a means to travel the world and see places that he had only dreamed of. A way to forget the hurt and disappointed expression on his father's face when he had told him he was leaving the farm. He never imagined that he would end up on an aircraft carrier, not only cooking the meals but growing the damned potatoes as well.

Corey laughed aloud, even though he couldn't hear the sound himself. The CD player that he had scavenged from the electronics shop three weeks ago, when he was told to collect batteries, was turned up full blast, Iron Maiden hammering at his ears. Another little something surviving from the Auld Sod, the British Isles. It was his secret guilt, that player, and it meant that he could tune out of the hum and bustle of the carrier; shut away the loud noises that echoed belowdecks through the monstrous behemoth.

Unfortunately for Corey it also meant that he hadn't heard the door in the south of the hangar deck creak open and then bang against the outer wall. He hadn't heard the slow footfalls of the visitor approaching him. If he had turned a few seconds earlier, he would have seen the dim UV lights casting shadows across the torn face that had once belonged to Aaron Carson – as the undead Preacher lumbered forward, dragging his left leg heavily across patches of spilt soil.

When the song that was playing on Corey's CD player ended and didn't jump to the next track, he looked down and tapped the device a few times, wondering if the batteries were finally going. It was then that he heard it – a low rattling rasp that cut through even the muffling of the headphones.

Corey spun around at the noise and took a step back, instinctively holding up the only weapon available to him at the time – a trowel – and felt his heart miss a beat.

This... it wasn't possible... not on the ship, not belowdecks. Not after all this time...

He took two more steps back, and stared straight into the dead face of the Preacher, who in turn glared back at him with a burning hatred that made Corey feel a chill down to his bootsoles. The Preacher. The one who took up the post of the disappeared chaplain. But this wasn't the same man. This was the dead version. This one had a gaping hole in his face and claw marks across his arms. This one opened its mouth and hissed, a sound of pure malice.

The creature reached for him, now only a few feet away, and Corey swung the trowel, hitting it in the neck just above the collarbone. Black blood splattered across the already wilting potato plants. The zombie lashed out, grasping Corey's shirt and pulling hard as he tried to escape, to clamber through the plant bed – but the weight of the corpse pulled him back and sent him stumbling. He tripped, called out, and dropped the trowel as he flailed his arms and tried to break his own fall. But he only had one hand to do it with.

I miss you, Dad, was the last thing that went

through Corey's mind as his head hit the wooden edge of the plant bed, knocking him cold instantly. Corey would not wake up again, at least not as Corey. Thirty seconds later his system began shutting down and going into shock, as the virus spread rapidly through his system. He hadn't even felt the bite in his arm that had been the catalyst, hadn't even noticed the clumsy figure stumbling away across the hangar toward the north door. He also didn't sense others pass him by as he lay there dying.

Ten minutes later, Corey Westrow rose, sniffed at the air, and started shuffling in the same direction. Around him others staggered through the plant beds as the sound of gunfire began echoing through the corridors. But now he barely heard those noises. All that went through Corey's dead mind was pure instinct, pure hatred, and a single impulse.

Feed.

JUMP MASTER

The wind and stinging rain slapped Captain Ainsley in the face like it had gotten a good wind-up, and lightning flashes rippled in 360 degrees. He was immediately disoriented in the black cloud soup, tumbling and trying to maintain his breathing through his regulator.

This was the worst weather he had ever jumped into. Never mind from high altitude.

He had of course gone out the door first, leading from the front. Anything else would have been unthinkable for a combat leader – in USOC, in the SAS, or in any regiment.

As senior NCO, Command Sergeant Major Handon would be jumping last, tail-gunner Charlie, riding herd on his flock.

But even now, the others would be tumbling out right behind Ainsley, and despite the horrifying conditions, he had to be effective, and he had to hit his marks. He spared one look for the altimeter, none for the GPS, and deployed his canopy. Within a few seconds, he began to spot the flashing IR beacons of the others, which made bright and pretty green fireflies in his night-vision goggles.

With a little luck and timing, they'd be ditching the NVGs within half an hour. By the time they hit

Chicago, coming in west from across Lake Michigan, as well as down from the sky, sunlight should be breaking. Or maybe, once underneath the cloud cover, there'd at least be gloom they could see through.

Visuals were dodgy, so Ainsley did a radio head count. No one below would be listening. Everyone sounded off. He checked his instruments again, and everything checked. So, following his compass, he turned his canopy on the proper heading, and felt as much as saw the seven others maintain formation around him.

And right now all they had to do was fly thirty miles to Chicago... but it was after they hit the ground that things would get tricky.

* * *

Handon didn't much like it. But, then again, as so often, he didn't have to like it — he just had to do it. The weather was a bastard. But he and his people could make it happen anyway.

He felt the weight of his leg bag hanging beneath him. When he hit the drop zone, the parachute canopy would come off — and the leg bag would convert to his ruck. For now, to ensure a common rate of descent of all the gliding paratroopers, gear had been carefully apportioned to keep everyone the same weight.

If all went well, they'd cover the 32,000 or so feet

of descent to the height of their target structure, and the 30 miles to downtown Chicago, in about 34 minutes.

But it couldn't be said that everything was going well so far.

Just maintaining formation was a nearly full physical and cognitive load on all the operators, as they were buffeted mercilessly by the storm. Plus, with the temperature lower than predicted, and the higher wind chill, hypothermia was becoming a real risk – they lost about 2.6 degrees Fahrenheit for every 1,000 feet of altitude. And as the extremities began to go numb, their ability to manipulate the canopy, or any other equipment, dropped toward zero.

Handon saw one of the IR beacons ahead of him begin to veer dramatically, the operator it represented sucked off course by a rogue gust of wind in the storm. He was pretty sure he knew who it was.

"Ali, sitrep," he said into his throat mic.

Since she weighed the least of anyone in the group, her leg bag was the heaviest – which left her with the lowest power-to-weight ratio of any of them. She was having to battle her steering lines, with her lesser upper-body strength. And as the storm picked up, and the cold sucked her strength and dexterity, she was losing the battle.

"*I've got it,*" she said. Sure enough, the wayward beacon began slowly, tremblingly, to merge with the group again.

What Handon had forgotten, but never should have, is that strength is a puny factor compared to the one that defines a special operator:

Resolve.

And which Ali had in greater measure than any other soldier Handon had ever met.

He thought he could now begin to make out the edge, of dark on slightly less dark, where the shore of the Great Lake met the Windy City. Somewhere a few hundred meters inland would be the tiny rooftop upon which they had to land.

Some fucking aircraft beacon lights, he thought, *would come in handy right about now.*

Instead they were going to have to rely on GPS.

And, if that went out, on visual landmarks and dead reckoning.

Hell of a way to start the day, Handon thought.

Below him, in his imagination, the city seemed to moan.

INSURRECTION

Wesley was already waking drowsily, when he woke violently to the sound of an explosion. Surely it was only in his dream? His dreams had been getting worse, not helped by the claustrophobia of sleeping in a sailor's berth. Worst of all, opening his eyes did nothing – the world was just as black on the other side of them. The sound of gunfire – rattlingly, crashingly, pummellingly loud and echoing in the steel confines of the ship-city's belly – told him that the explosion had not been in his dreams.

Thank fuck, the lights now came on – revealing Martin in his skivvies, standing at the switch, by the door. The two men shared a disbelieving look. The sound of gunfire, in at least two calibers, shook the room. Martin reached for the door handle. Wesley's mouth went wide, trying to find the words to make him stop, but it was too late.

Martin pulled the door wide enough for them both to see angry green tracers skipping down the hall in both directions, like lethal fireflies at light-speed in the near dark.

Martin pushed the door shut again, then retreated back to his bunk, and began shakily pulling his clothes on. Wesley mimicked him. *Better to die dressed, I guess*, he thought... Captain Martin also found his sidearm, drew it, chamber-checked that there was a round loaded, then wrapped the belt with the holster around his waist.

Wesley sidled closer, and found his voice. "What in hell's going on?"

"I have absolutely no idea," Martin said. Then he did have an idea. He found his mobile and speed-dialed Drake. It rang through to voicemail. Martin rang off and dialed again. On the third attempt, it answered. *"Go for Drake!"* The man was shouting – over gunfire.

"Drake, Captain Martin. What the bloody hell is going on?"

There was a pause, with more gunfire, before an answer came. *"Mutiny! It's the fucking Zealots. They've got numbers, arms, and surprise. They've taken the goddamned Bridge and are trying to run the ship aground."*

"Where are you?" Martin asked, his face a mask of dismay.

"We're in the island, mostly scattered around the Launch Ops Room and the Flag Bridge. We're trying to retake the Bridge. Fuck it. Never mind. Stay put. Arm yourselves if possible. I'll come for you when I can. Out."

The line went dead. Martin regarded the phone before him.

The door to the room flew open. Martin dropped the phone, raised his sidearm, and nearly shot the man who came through it. It was one of the MARSOC Marines, cradling a .45-caliber H&K UMP sub-machine gun and appearing slightly wounded.

After almost shooting Martin in turn, he surveyed the room. "You're the Brits."

Martin and Wesley both nodded.

"You loyal to this vessel?"

They both nodded again, more vigorously. "God, yes," Wesley stammered.

The Marine nodded his acceptance of this. "Stay put. Don't open this door." Then he stepped back into the passageway, one hand on his weapon, the other on the hatch handle to pull it closed. A round took him in the head and knocked him over backward.

He lay dead and still on the deck before Martin – who suddenly got an overwhelming sense that this deck wasn't in fact going to be retaken. "Come on," he said to Wesley. "I think we're going to be overrun if we stay here."

Wesley had to swallow an enormous bolus of fear before he could make himself step out that hatch.

* * *

They went the direction the Marine hadn't gotten shot from. Soon they were amongst running throngs of sailors, and the odd Marine, who were scrambling, loading weapons, shouting at one another, and trying to figure out what the hell was going on.

"Well?" Wesley shouted over the tumult. "What now?"

"I say let's go find Drake. I think I can get us to

the island from here."

Wesley wasn't sure that was the best idea he'd heard all morning, but that route at least seemed to take them away from the fighting belowdecks. Or so they thought – the route Martin knew took them first up to the flight deck, which they'd then have to cross to get to the island.

Martin poked his head up over the ladder first. He could hear gunfire from the direction of the island – and every few seconds a stray tracer would flash off into the dimness of the gray and heavily overcast morning. From the wind coursing over the flight deck, and the sound of the surf, the ship seemed to be moving, and moving briskly.

Just as Martin gave Wesley the (more or less) all clear, and they both clambered up onto deck, a raucous and terrifying explosion rocked the outer edge of the deck, knocking them halfway back down the hatch again. Much of the world to their right went up in an orange and white inferno, which briefly lit up nearly every inch of the deck like stage lighting, tore a hole in the cloudy sky, and totally seared the vision and hearing of the two refugees.

"What the fuck was that?!" Wesley shouted, looking away and covering his eyes.

Martin was no expert, but he clocked the location as being that of the starboard Sparrow missile launchers. "A weapons magazine, I think!"

"Jesus Christ! Is this safe?!"

Martin realized that was very much a question worth considering.

But then he spotted the flaming figures lurching toward them across the deck – from right out of the flames at the site of the explosion.

For just one second, he thought they were wounded and burning sailors.

But then he recognized that walk.

"*Ruuunnn!*" he shouted, pulling Wesley up the ladder, and both of them into a headlong flight toward the island.

Wesley went with it and came up running, hand over head – but he spared a look over his shoulder trying to make out their pursuers. "What?" he stammered, "what is it?"

"*It's the dead, you fool...!*"

A long hundred meters lay between them and that island.

Bullets began snapping the air over their heads.

And urgent moaning grew louder behind them.

DROP ZONE

Ainsley's GPS fix was coming on and off. On the upside, the storm was starting to blow itself out, clearing from in front of a strong wind off the lake – or what was really a large inland sea posing as a lake. The captain and Alpha commander squinted to get a visual on the target building. He began flaring his chute and hauling on his steering lines to get himself and his team on a heading that would intersect it, before he was too low and on an express elevator for the probable wild west of street level. The others, slightly behind and above him, had a little more space and time, and thus a little more room to maneuver.

Ainsley fought a stiff tailwind from off the lake, as it tried to push him past the drop zone. The rooftop was coming up fast, and Ainsley, and all of them, were still too far to the north of it. Ainsley's biceps strained against his lines like the reins of a runaway stagecoach, and his face beaded sweat, despite the chill air. He, and the others, had all ditched the oxygen masks as they passed through 7,000 feet.

He spared a look behind him. The formation was slightly ragged, but they all seemed more or less on the same vector. As to whether he was going to be able to master both the wind and gravity in time to make the drop zone... The cluttered rooftop raced toward him on three axes – left, forward, and down – and Ainsley hauled on his left riser for all he was worth.

The wind slackened slightly and the building finally lined up under him. They were going to make it. Ainsley flared his canopy at the last second to slow his rate of descent; a broken leg or other serious landing injury would really mess up everyone's day. But his descent instantly slowed *much* more than he'd intended – reversed in fact, lifting him back up into the sky.

It was a massive updraft, driven by the low-pressure zone left by the storm, fed by the warm air off the lake, and coming up the vertical cliffside of the building. Ainsley found himself rising radically, while still moving forward – the updraft was going to take him right over the edge of the building. He was going to miss the rooftop entirely.

Nothing else to be done, and no time to do anything else anyway. Pulling the quick releases on his canopy, he fell from the chute and plummeted straight down, more than twenty feet to the hard rooftop. On landing, he still had forward momentum, and rolled into it, hoping to absorb the force across his side and shoulder. While desperately trying to survive his landing, he was also completely aware that he had no idea what was happening to the rest of his team.

Until, that is, everyone started shouting into their team radios at once.

The squad net had gone completely hectic.

And Ainsley tumbled toward the building edge end over end – a tangle of man, equipment, and webbing.

* * *

Predator initially kept his mouth shut and off the radio. He wasn't one for sending traffic when things in his sector went to shit. It was too much like whining. He preferred to deal with a crisis and then bring the others up to speed as and when. Of course, there was a fine line between operating independently and neglecting team comms and coordination. But very often there was just no time, and that was the case now.

The same updraft that blindsided Ainsley caught him – but higher and farther from the target building. He tried to steer to correct, but after the towering wave of air took him to its apex, a crosswind caught his big body and bigger canopy, and slung him off to the side like a rock in a sling. For the moment, he was basically out of control, and watched the next rooftop, maybe five stories lower than the target, race at him at train-wreck speed.

He figured now might be an okay time to radio something in. "Uh... Pred going in hard. Mayday, motherfuckers..."

The surface of this other building's roof was a tangle of antennas, satellite dishes, and duct pipes.

One particularly tall radio tower, which probably had the building's aircraft warning light, back when there were lights, looked like having Predator's number on it. As he whirled in a spiral beneath and outside of his canopy, he thought to himself:

Yeah… this is gonna hurt.

* * *

Juice had been descending less than twenty meters behind and above Predator. But due to the vagaries of micro-weather and low-pressure systems, the updraft that caught his friend left him in peace. He was still working hard to control his flight and descent, but he was on a solid vector for their drop zone – when everything went to shit.

He saw Ainsley, in the lead, head up toward the troposphere – then drop right out from under his canopy. He lost track of him after that, as his gaze snapped to the right – where Predator was doing some kind of para-gyroscope routine, spiraling down into the next building over. His final rotation took his lines dead across a tall radio tower. After that, his rate of spin increased, wrapping tightly around it. He stopped when his body smacked into its side with a crack so loud it was audible above the wind, and a hundred yards away.

He came to rest hanging upside down by his lines, fouled in risers and soggy chute. The weight of his kit bag levered his leg at a sickeningly unnatural angle.

And that was as far as Juice had time to follow it. Because he also had to decide on his own course of action in an instant, and did so – hauling on his right steering line, coming around, passing over the edge of the target building, and soaring down toward its neighbor. He flared two seconds later, coming to rest perfectly upright, both feet planted, a textbook landing, totally squared away.

Just on the wrong building.

His big reddish-brown beard twitched beneath his black tactical helmet as he sniffed loudly, once, then paused in that spot for a single second.

Then he shrugged out of his harness while drawing a six-inch Spyderco knife from his chest harness, used it to cut free his leg bag, then advanced with the knife through the gloom toward his friend. If there turned out to be any Zulus up here with them, well, he figured he'd just have to deal with them the old fashioned way. He flipped the enormous knife up onto the back of his hand, then palmed it again.

Overhand grip – right down through the top of the skull.

* * *

Ali's final approach was going pretty well, actually – until Ainsley's released and now free-flying chute came flapping back at her through the damp gloom like Mothra in some kind of gray and storm-tossed hell. Only a decade and a half of intensive training and operational experience in disaster management allowed her to keep her cool.

If that chute hit her anywhere – her body, her lines, or especially her own canopy – she'd be fouled and mostly likely fall out of the sky like a meat rock. She yanked on both lines with every ounce of her strength, flaring and turning. At the last second, she tensed and pulled both her knees into her chest. (*Thank fuck for all that ab work…*) The snapping, splashing, whistling mass of parachute slipped beneath her with inches to spare.

Having survived that, and getting her bearings, her next crisis was obvious: having slowed her descent to dodge the chute, she'd overshot the target building. She sailed now into the canyon of skyscrapers with no building tops of any sort any longer in her line of sight… and beneath her nothing but the major artery of West Lake Street.

Nothing but the near death-sentence of street level.

She got on the squad net, speaking normally. "Ali to Command. I have overshot drop zone. Repeat, overshot drop zone. My new location is about to be, uh… *downtown*. Stand by."

No, scratch that about there being only the street below. There was also the Chicago River, which was only now resolving to her through the near darkness. And also the elevated train platform, providing a complex hazard thirty feet *above* the hard street.

And both of those were coming up pretty damned fast, too.

* * *

Homer was perfectly in the pipe himself, set to hit his marker with precision.

But then he saw everything go wrong. He saw it all: Ainsley's rise and fall, Pred's whirl-a-gig, Juice's diversion – and Ali's death-defyingly close call. And then her sailing off toward downtown. It was all laid out before and below him, like box seats to an opera of fatal errors.

And he decided his own fate in a second as well. Their orders from the pre-mission briefings were completely clear – force protection was *not* a mission priority. Nobody went back for anyone else. Everyone went forward toward the mission objective – no matter what. But…

There was no way Homer could make himself leave Ali on that street alone. Not at this point, not after everything. No, he'd much sooner die down there with her, than listen to her die from the safety of a rooftop. This loved one he was coming for – no matter what.

Heck with it, he figured in his own head. *Guess I'm just not in an order-following mood today…*

He flared early, overshot the rooftop with plenty of room to spare, and followed her down.

He figured he'd update command on that one

when he got where he was going.

* * *

Handon, Henno, and Pope, at various points up on the actual target rooftop, got out of their harnesses, charged their weapons, and got to Ainsley at about the same time. There was a wire fence that ringed the rooftop, and protected anyone up there from a 24-story fall. But Ainsley had crashed through it – with his helmet.

Now his head and shoulders stuck out into open air, hundreds of feet above the cement. He seemed lucid, but not quite ready to try moving. Henno and Pope each grabbed a leg and pulled him back in, while Handon faced behind them, took a knee, put his rifle to his shoulder, and pulled security. Parachuting accidents didn't mean the enemy wasn't going to show up, or would give you a time-out.

"Sitrep," Ainsley said, sitting up and shaking his head. He also rubbed his left shoulder, where he had taken much of the force of the fall.

The four of them pieced together what had happened, and worked out everyone's current, or probable, location. This project was aided when Juice and Homer reported in from their improvised rescue ops.

"Right," Ainsley said, climbing shakily to his feet. "So I guess it's just disobey fucking orders day, then, isn't it…"

Pope and Henno dealt with distributing the combat load in the leg bags, while Ainsley and Handon tried to put together a plan to salvage the mission.

Or at least to keep all their people alive through the next few minutes.

ALL OVER THE PLACE / NO PLACE

"Roger that, Top," Juice said, after briefing Handon over the radio, and getting general instructions from him in turn. "What I'll do is strongpoint here for now, while I see about Pred's mobility – and then look at options for getting down off this building." He grabbed the top of his head to scratch his scalp with his ballcap – but found only his tactical helmet, which was strapped down tight and didn't shift. "Yeah, we're always careful. Yeah, just like church mice… Juice out."

He went down on one knee, just in front of where Predator lay flat on his back. This was after Juice had cut him free, lowered him to the ground with sheer arm and back strength – and then straightened his right leg out for him. The brittle cracking sound had only been audible because Predator had declined to scream. He'd also declined morphine.

Juice waggled a syrette of morphine sulfate in front of his face, which was drenched with sweat. "Ready for some of that sweet fruit of the poppy now, tough guy?"

Predator snatched it and crushed it in his hand. The oozing liquid did smell sweet, like vanilla. Pred tossed it away and wiped his hand on his assault suit. "You show me another one of those, you son of a bitch, and you and me are going to have words."

Juice wasn't surprised. Giant unstoppable badasses like Predator generally preferred to bull through pain, rather than dull their senses and reflexes mid-mission. Though it was looking an awful lot like Pred's mission was over before it had begun.

"All right," Juice said, knowing it was totally pointless to argue. "You sit tight. Gonna check the roof access." As he hefted his SIG assault rifle, he saw Pred draw one of his .45 pistols and lay it across his chest. Juice stepped off into the sooty maze of the rooftop. The sun was just cracking on the horizon somewhere out there, and the morning lightening.

After doing a full circuit of the roof, rifle at low ready, he quickly found the two roof-access doors, most likely to emergency stairwells. Circling back to the first one, he tried rattling the doorknob. Locked. That of course could be fixed. He tried knocking lightly. Nothing. Back to the second door. He rattled the knob. Locked. He pulled back his gloved hand to try knocking.

The doorknob rattled, from the other side.

As he leapt backward like an electroshock victim, eyes going wide, the whole door began shaking violently in its frame. Juice stopped his backward lurch, solidified his stance, and used biofeedback techniques to bring his breathing and heart rate back down.

As much as he and Pred wanted off this rooftop… clearly, someone badly wanted in.

Predator came in over the squad net, from across the rooftop. The noise of the rattling door had obviously carried. *"Dude, what the fuck? Over."*

* * *

Ainsley and Handon stood off to one side, in conference. Their situation was slowly clarifying. And it seemingly got worse with every revelation, with every decision point they had to consider.

"So what's your call?" Handon asked.

Ainsley looked grim. "I think we need to get the QRF moving." Handon raised his eyebrows at that. Ainsley persisted. "We've got one wounded, one missing, and two separated, at exactly H-hour plus zero seconds. We're already down to half strength."

Handon shrugged. "True. But on the other hand, we're not in contact yet. And we're guaranteed to be if those Sea Hawks come screaming in here." If the QRF launched now, they'd have to do it in the helos – their prop plane wouldn't reach the carrier again for another two hours.

Ainsley nodded. "We could execute the waterborne infil option." This contingency plan called for the MARSOC team to put down in rigid inflatable boats a mile out in Lake Michigan, then motor in.

Handon didn't look impressed. "With the storm over, plus the wind off the lake, I'm afraid the engine noise would still carry. And if it didn't, those Zodiac engines would when they got near the shoreline. I say we just get on with it."

Ainsley seemed as if he was starting to see it his way.

"And I can't raise the *JFK* anyway."

"What?" Ainsley's eyebrows went for his helmet.

"Just now, trying to radio in our status. No answer to my hails. Nothing."

"No signal — from the top of a 24-story building?"

Handon just held his gaze. They both knew this was another very bad portent.

* * *

Parachuting right down through the skyscraper canyons of a major city was actually the extreme-sports experience of a lifetime. *Wish I were in a position to give a shit*, Ali considered.

She also considered the Hobson's choice that now confronted her. On her current heading and speed, she was going in the drink. Ditching it in the Chicago River in late November would without question mean dicing with hypothermia. When she got out of the water — that's if she could cut loose from enough gear to swim, plus find a section of embankment not too sheer for her to climb up — she'd have maybe an hour to get undressed and dried out. After that, she was a goner.

And before that, out on the street, alone, with all of her weapons and equipment gone, she was also a goner.

Even braking her forward momentum against the tailwind, and speeding her rate of descent as much as she dared, she didn't think she could get down on the main drag. And her forward speed was too high, and her turning radius too wide, to try and just turn down a side street.

What did that leave? That left the 'L' – as they called the elevated train platform that circled the Loop, right near the edge of the river. It perched over the street, directly between her and the water. Normal skydiving instincts had led her to steer away from this at all costs – wildly uneven surface, dangerously high above ground, electrified. Fucking *trains* coming. On any normal, non-apocalyptic jump, this would be the absolute worst conceivable place to land.

Now it was looking like her only hope.

Hell, it's actually looking pretty sweet, she amended. Up off the street. Probably no longer electrified. And certainly no trains coming.

Now – all she had to do was avoid snapping part or all of herself off in the tracks while landing.

* * *

Homer worked out what Ali was doing too late. Coming over the top of the target building with more control, he'd had time to think about avoiding both the water and the 'L', and to brake himself toward a street landing in front of both hazards.

And not only had he failed to mentally re-evaluate the implications of landing on the train platform, but he'd also reconciled himself to facing whatever he would find down there on the street. In his own mind, he was already dead. And now he'd already lost too much altitude to bring it back up and follow Ali.

The street was in deep darkness – the sun hadn't cracked the horizon down here yet – and all that black space now loomed, racing up at him, with whatever it held, and all it hid.

* * *

The half of Alpha team that had actually made it to the intended landing zone now stacked up outside the rooftop-access door of the target building. This meant the four of them stood in a tight line down the side of the wall, Pope in the lead. Ordinarily a door stack and dynamic entry would mean blowing the door with a small charge, shooting it off its hinges with shotgun slugs, or bashing it in with a mechanical breaching tool. Also, a couple of flashbang grenades would precede their entry – which would then turn into a swirling maelstrom of controlled chaos. They would pour in and clear the structure, making shoot/no-shoot decisions, executing four-box shots on the shoots, and taking down and controlling the no-shoots.

That was how they'd done it back in the world.

In this after-world, though… everything they faced would (almost) definitely be a shoot; flashbangs didn't really work; and noise just brought more of them. So Pope squatted down, withdrew two small tools from a small folding leather case, and picked the lock. He pulled the door open quickly but quietly.

The other three, NVGs seated on the fronts of their helmets again, slithered into the interior darkness. Pope followed, pulled the door shut… and locked it behind them.

* * *

In the final moment before impact, Ali saw what she hadn't before: a blessed train station. It was two bits of roof over the platform, and looked a hell of a lot more promising as a landing surface than the bare tracks. She hauled for all she was worth, brought it around at the last instant, and executed a running, sliding landing on the tiled but nearly horizontal surface.

She skidded to a stop, well pleased with herself.

As she reached for her chute quick release, the ground (i.e. the roof) opened up from under her. She fell with a crash, right through the rotten structure, and twelve feet to the hard wooden platform below. On her way through, a spike-shaped shard of wood went in one side of her left bicep and came out the other. She landed on her back, stunned, bleeding from the arm, and vertebrae screaming. Her rifle was wedged painfully beneath her. Her leg bag came down on top of her in a spray of dust and rotted wood, knocking the remaining wind out of her.

She drew a lungful of air with spectacular difficulty, rolled off her rifle, charged it with her right hand, and dragged both it and herself away from the center of the platform and up to the outside wall of the station office. She then sat still, in complete silence, amid crashing waves of pain, tuning into the environment and waiting.

Waiting to see what would come for her.

* * *

Pope, Ainsley, Henno, and Handon now stacked up a second time – this time outside the emergency stairwell door on floor 18. Behind it would be the offices of NeuraDyne Neurosciences. They had encountered no resistance on the way down from the roof. This was surprising, but they didn't show it. Their job was to be completely ready for anything. And that included when they faced absolutely nothing.

This time Pope had to jimmy the door's one-way locking bar with a thin metal rod. It gave with a metallic pop. Ainsley pushed his way in, rifle barrel and binocular NVGs pointing ahead of him like the prow of a military spaceship. The other three slithered inside after him.

In three minutes, they had cleared the level.

There was nothing there.

No living, no dead. Just a small bit of detritus that seemed to indicate people here had cleared out in a hurry. And two years of dust on the carpet and desk surfaces.

"And no fucking computers," Handon said, flipping up his NVGs and yanking the blinds away from the exterior windows, which let in a bit of thin early-morning light. From the large-screen LCDs and docking stations at most of the desks, it was obvious everyone here had worked off laptops. Which were now just as gone as the people were.

Pope stepped back into the main office area. "I've scoured the labs. No machines, no servers. And it looks like most of the samples and slides have done a runner."

Ainsley cursed silently under his breath. *All this way, and a dry hole…*

Henno called to them from the reception area. "Oi. I found some e-mail."

Ainsley was opening his mouth to ask how the hell he could have found e-mail when there were no blighting computers for it to be on… But Henno was already walking into the room. With his gloved hand, he held out a single piece of A4 paper. Ainsley took it.

It was a one-page e-mail print-out.

DEAD CITY

After a perfect two-point landing in the dead middle of the street, Homer trotted to a halt, reeled in his chute, shrugged out of his harness, wrapped the latter in the former, and shoved the whole bundle down an open street drain. He then unslung his weapon, charged it, grabbed his leg bag by its strap with his left hand, and got the hell off the street.

This meant ducking into a recessed doorway. He immediately took a very careful gander through the windows for any sign of movement inside, then put his full attention back on the street. His patrol boots, sleek and form-fitting assault suit and load-bearing harness, short-barrelled assault rifle, and hockey-style tactical helmet melted fluidly into the dim recess. He looked out, pivoting from his left, to his right, to directly across the way. Nothing moved in the lightening gloom.

That's not so bad, then. He almost smiled at his good luck so far.

But then he grimaced again. This was supposed to be a city of three million dead people. Where in God's name were they all? He should be neck-deep right now. He felt reprieved. But he also felt a sense of deep foreboding. Something was very wrong. And it couldn't, in the end, turn out to be good.

All around him, littering the street, were the telltale signs of a struggle for survival long lost. There were no fresh bodies. Two years of Chicago weather had seen to that, and all that remained were rag-covered bones littering the ground. A few feet away, in the next doorway along, were two adult-sized skeletons clutching each other. Homer stared at them for a moment and wondered what this place had been like the day those two huddled in that doorway for shelter.

He scanned the area, looking a second time for movement. But apart from the bits of trash that littered the street, skittering in the slight wind, nothing moved.

He pressed the transmit button built into the foregrip of his assault rifle and hailed Ali.

She hadn't been quite so lucky in her landing, he learned in short order. She was working to keep the pain out of her voice, with some success. But the effort was costing her.

Homer told her to stay put, signed off, and immediately picked up her grid location from his forearm-mounted Blue Force Tracker. The transponder in her BFT unit was talking seamlessly with his. She was close – but not close enough for comfort, and also elevated. The moving map in his forearm-mounted display drew out a route for him.

He moved out smartly, hugging the walls and building fronts. Back in the world before, this was a no-no – bullets also hugged walls, sometimes skimming along them for hundreds of feet, making them an excellent place to get shot. But now, of course, no one was shooting back – and the great thing was to stay out of sight, and silent. This was often made easier, as it was in this dead city, by the abandoned cars and garbage that lay everywhere.

The streets were quiet through his short journey, as Homer skirted his way along the sidewalk, ducking behind cars, posts, and trash cans, and keeping to doorways – though only the ones that were still more or less intact. Open doorways were to be avoided at all costs, especially if the building they led to was in darkness. Which all these were.

He'd had a few close moments making that mistake back in the early days. Zombies didn't tend to deliberately hide themselves away – they weren't clever enough for that – but they often wandered into a building when catching the scent of the living, and then stayed there in the dark if nothing else caught their attention. With walls around them, they seemed to find it hard to navigate their way out. All of this meant that the open front of a house, shop, or other structure represented a pretty high risk of something coming sprawling out at you. And standing in the doorway, with sunlight in your eyes and low visibility into the building, was a good way to get yourself jumped and chomped.

Homer moved swiftly from cover to cover, still wondering why the hell there weren't any signs of the dead – signs of anything for that matter. But within a block, the silence gave way. He squatted down, frozen, making himself small, as soon as he heard it. It was just up ahead, and unmistakable – but so out of place that he struggled to comprehend it.

Finally he realized: it was music.

He blinked hard and stayed where he was, willing himself not to go mad.

* * *

"Roger that, I'm not going anywhere," Ali said, in response to Homer's hail. "Walk safely. Out."

Jesus Christ, Homer… This was some damned unprofessionalism right here, following her down in her missed drop. Still, all things considered, she couldn't say she minded the assistance. She was in a bit of a bad way.

She popped a handful of analgesics from her med kit. She'd already pulled the wood splinter – "spike" was more like it – from her arm, let it bleed freely for a bit, then disinfected and wrapped it up. It hurt like hell, and the arm felt out of commission for the duration. Luckily, sniping was mostly done one-handed – with the off hand resting across the shooting arm for stability. She followed the Diclofenac pills with a jab – full-spectrum antibiotics, also from the med kit, and directly into her impaled arm. There was no telling what disgusting shit was on that roof after two years. Pigeon crap might be the best of it.

She'd also wrenched her back badly. But outside of a hospital, or probably a sports rehab clinic, there was nothing she could do but endure it. Now that she was basically squared away, she had to decide whether to sit tight and wait for rescue – or get up and make herself useful.

Well, she thought, clenching her jaw, *I guess that one answers itself.*

* * *

Homer faced a decision point as well, and it was also auto-answering. However spooky the next few meters, they had to be crossed. He leg-pressed himself up out of his deep crouch, rifle at his shoulder, and started taking one padded step after another.

Dear Lord, he thought. *What madness was this?* Chicago was supposed to be a dead city. There was *no way* there was power generation still on here. Not two years later. And he figured a live band had to be out of the question.

Step by creeped-out step, he heard the music grow louder, until it was clearly audible.

"Wait 'til you're locked in my embrace," the velvet voice crooned. *"Wait 'til I hold you near... Wait 'til you see that sunshine place...There ain't nothin' like it here..."*

Homer knew the song well: Frank Sinatra, "The Best Is Yet To Come." Maybe that was even more ironic than "My Kind of Town" would have been?

Who could say. Not Homer.

On closer approach, he found it was floating out of a storefront jazz joint and cocktail bar. He stepped slowly through a set of swing doors that hung from the entrance, broken as though someone had tried to rip them off the wall and failed. One of the doors was covered in black stains that could have been zombie or dried-up human blood. He couldn't tell. Moving inside, he scanned all the dark spots and covered positions as he advanced. Nothing moved, but all over the floor were desiccated human remains, much of it chaotically scattered.

They really tore this place apart, he thought.

In short order, he determined that the music was coming from satellite speakers along the walls – and found them all connected to a digital jukebox behind the bar. The jukebox was plugged into the same socket as a nearby fridge. Slowly pulling its door open, Homer found that it was full of beer bottles – full beer bottles, not opened ones. And the fridge was still on, though the light bulb had long since burned out. Also plugged into the socket via a three-way adapter was something that looked like a mini vehicle battery, though it was too small to be a standard car battery. It was wired up to a standard plug, as if being recharged. Homer wondered if someone had come here after the city had fallen, or if this had been here before. He would never know. Nothing else lived in the establishment. And nothing else had power. It was just a complete mystery.

Homer paused at the front door before leaving. *Not a mystery*, he thought.

A miracle.

* * *

Ali cleared both train platforms, as well as the Chicago Transit Authority offices on either side, in four minutes. Her arm hurt like hell, and her back a lot worse than that, but she retained most of her mobility. She held her rifle by resting it on her left forearm. When she got back to her starting point, and her leg bag, she flipped down the rifle's bipod, and popped the cover on the big scope.

And she had a think about where she might emplace to best effect up here.

* * *

The Miracle of St. Frank, Homer thought, back on the street now, and beyond bemused. The real miracle, of course, and as he well knew, was that the music had not drawn zombie one. It should have been like catnip for them at this point. Where were all the dead? As he moved out and forward, on a hair trigger, ready for anything... still he encountered nothing.

When he reached the 'L' station, only a minute or so later, he had to stop to recalibrate. All of the stairwells leading up to the platform had been destroyed. This was not unusual. Alpha had been on the scenes of very many last stands. In addition to the bullet casings, the wide splashes of blood, the broken windows and toppled doors, one great hallmark of a human last stand was destroyed first-floor stairwells. Anyone smart enough to think of it, and with the tools or strength to manage it, did this. It was one of the best strategies for keeping the dead away the longest.

He reported the lack of access to Ali. "But be advised, I'll find a way to climb up..." He was already up and moving along underneath the platform, looking for egress. "Just stay put."

"*Negative*," she transmitted back. "*This is actually an excellent sniper's OP. And if you can sweep and clear the street directly below me, I think we can be pretty effective.*"

Homer stopped where he was, his eyes narrowing. "Effective at what?"

In answer, Ali's suppressed rifle chugged twice from over his head.

He spun in place and took cover. He couldn't see what she was shooting at. But it wouldn't be nothing... "*Contact, due south*," came her inevitable report. "*Visual on multiple Zulus, approx one-zero, in ones and twos. And they are closing distance.*"

* * *

Ainsley scanned the printed e-mail, the other three standing still in the dim and dusty room. It was addressed to roughly fifty recipients. About half the addresses sounded like other biotechs or university labs, about half perhaps personal contacts. He read it aloud:

I pray to God most or all of you receive this. If you're still online, I don't have to tell you how bad things are. Virtually all of my colleagues have gone now - back to their families, or their homes in the country, or to whatever fate awaits them out there.

I can actually see the fighting going on in buildings across the street. And I know it's only a matter of time before they are here as well.

I have stayed, to continue the work. We're so close, to either a vaccine, or an antidote, or both, so close I can taste it... the samples we have are excellent, and I know we can do it, given enough time. But I don't think I can stay here. To do so would simply be to wait for death.

Some of you know my brother-in-law, Al, who is an IT contractor. After 9/11, they put in a bunker beneath the Chicago Mercantile Exchange, beneath the trading floor. It was supposed to allow them to keep operating during a natural or man-made disaster. They've got generator power, food and water, I don't know how long for. Maybe weapons, too, I don't know. I know all this because Al worked on the project, on the security and IT systems. I also know there's a backdoor - literal, and figurative. There's a tunnel entrance that comes out in the basement of the Hyatt, across the street from the Mercantile Exchange Center. It's behind an unmarked steel door with a keypad, card reader, and thumbprint reader. It normally requires both a smartcard and a recognized thumbprint, in addition to a code. But Al programmed in a backdoor: if you just type 19 zeros in a row, it opens up. Obviously, I'm not supposed to know any of this. If I make it there, and I get in, maybe those already inside will shoot me. But that actually sounds much better than the remaining alternatives at this point.

The Exchange is close, only about six blocks from here. Maybe I can make it. I'm taking a laptop with all of the research data, as well as the samples, and some instruments, in a backpack. If you're in Chicago, and alive, and you get this, and you can make your way there, and you don't have any better options... well, it's a chance. And if you're a colleague elsewhere... if I make it there alive, and can continue working, and can somehow convey any results to you from there, I will.

May God protect you all.

Simon

"Well," said Henno, his palm on the butt of his sidearm. "That's some good luck, then."

Pope just shook his head at him. He had to hand it to that guy... everything always coming up roses in his world.

"Give me a map," Ainsley said, snapping his fingers at Handon, who pulled a digital map pack from a thigh pouch and handed it over. Ainsley powered it up and put it on the table, then zoomed and scrolled with thumb and forefinger. "Six block radius," he said, making a circle with both hands. "Chicago Mercantile Exchange Center... Hyatt..." he recited aloud while scanning. "Here." His finger came to rest on a spot four blocks south of their position, and two to the west. He keyed his transmit button and hailed Ali. Her traffic with Homer had been coming in loud and clear on the squad net from down on the street.

"*Ali here, you are Lima Charlie, send traffic,*" she answered.

"Interrogative: where are those Zulus of yours coming in from?"

"*The south, and a bit west. But they're not Zulus.*"

"What are they then?" Ainsley looked impatient.

"*I think they're Foxtrots. They've gotten extremely feisty since they've twigged to my presence up here, and to Homer down on the street.*"

"Copy that. Interrogative: how many Foxtrots, over."

After Ali pressed transmit, but before she answered, they could hear her suppressed rifle firing non-stop in the background. "*All of them, I think. Gotta bounce, Cap, these are SERIOUSLY hard shots to make. Out.*"

The three men looked to their officer. None of them looked worried.

But Captain Connor Ainsley sure as hell was. He nodded at Handon. "Okay. *Now* we call in the QRF. Do it." He knew that if it was a matter of fighting their way through the streets to a new location, they were going to need every gun they could get in the fight.

Handon twiddled his channel selector to the command net and hailed the *JFK* again.

And then again, and a third time. He just looked back up at Ainsley.

Nobody had to be told the new state of play.

They were on their own.

INSURRECTION][

Drake steadied his M4 rifle on the gunwale. He was kneeling on a balcony platform of the Flag Bridge, the second of the four habitable levels of the island. Directly above him was the Bridge; above that, Primary Flight Control; below him, at ground level, was the Flight Deck Control and Launch Operations Room. Drake was currently covering a rear sector in an unlikely battle, watching the flight deck below and behind them, as a mixed unit of sailors and Marines pressed forward to try and retake the Bridge.

But, frankly, it wasn't happening. The Zealots, the mutineers, had superior position, elevation, full control of the whole Bridge level of the island – and they had a lot of grenades. That made fighting their way back up there a tough row to hoe.

But Commander Drake knew they had somehow to do it. Only a few minutes after the bridge had been stormed and lost, the nuclear-powered steam turbines had blasted up to their full 320,000 horsepower, causing the whole vessel to vibrate. And then the four bronze screw propellers (each 22 feet across and weighing 68,000 pounds) began to spin. And then the whole mammoth vessel, all 110,000 tons of her, began to turn and to move.

And now she was steaming directly toward land. In what could be no more than twenty minutes, they would be run aground. At high speed, this would also likely rupture the hull, flooding the lower decks – and almost certainly putting the *Kennedy* out of action for the rest of time.

Clattering gunfire and throaty explosions shook the whole island. The bastards had come out of nowhere. No one had been expecting it. Standard shipboard security protocols had been in place for a combat mission in hostile waters, but these guys must have been planning this forever. And of course they knew all the security protocols, just as they knew everything else about how the ship was organized and run.

There had actually only ever been one mutiny in U.S. naval history, before this. And it had happened in 1842.

But, Drake considered, *I guess every damned thing's different now.*

Now he seemed to recall the SEAL, Homer, say something to that effect – that the interesting thing about a zombie apocalypse was what it did to the living. How they either worked together to survive – or else turned against each other, and clawed themselves to bits. With a painful twinge, he also remembered Homer trying to warn him about the Zealots. *Just too many damned things to worry about at once…*

And that's when the fore starboard Sparrow emplacement went up. *Jesus Christ…*

He saw two figures, backlit by the flames,

sprinting across the flight deck. Was it a Zealot counterattack, in their rear? Drake had secretly been relieved to not be on the front lines – it had been a long time since he qualified on the M4, though he kept up his pistol qualification. He pulled the assault rifle into his shoulder and took a bead on the lead figure down there… Oh, God, it was the British soldier… he eased up on the trigger, breathing hard.

And then he saw the burning figures behind them. And, like Martin, he soon recognized their motion – never mind that they weren't dying despite being covered head to toe in flame.

Mother of God, he thought, raising his barrel and taking a bead. He had no idea how it could possibly have happened, but now the dead were here. Out at sea, and in the middle of a raging insurrection. Fuck it. His first rounds caught one of them in the torso, slowing but not dropping it. He struggled to pull off a headshot. Underneath his barrel, he saw the Brits make it into the cover of the island.

While out on the flight deck, fires burned and the dead walked.

Drake frantically tried to figure out how they were going to keep them out of the island – while they were all still in the fight of their lives with the living for control of it…

* * *

Wesley and Martin leapt up the stairs, after a couple

of the loyalists one deck down directed them up. They found Drake out on his balcony, still sniping flaming corpse heads.

"I thought I told you to stay put?" he said.

"Apologies, Commander," Martin said. "Got too hot belowdecks." Wesley nodded rapidly in frantic agreement.

"Oh, hell." Drake's M4 stovepiped, and he stopped to try and clear the jam.

"Help you with that?" Martin asked. He took the weapon, promptly cleared and charged it, and took a couple of measured shots himself. He paused to hand his sidearm to Wesley, who seemed to know how to handle it. But now there were too many figures running around on the deck below: the mutineers, the loyalists, and the dead – who were loyal to no one. Some people shot others at close range, while others dove on and devoured them. It was complete and total chaos. Drake flinched and motioned them all inside.

"Look. We've all got to get in the fight upstairs," he said. "If we don't take the Bridge back within fifteen minutes, we're all completely screwed. We'll be run aground. Maybe sunk."

Martin nodded and took this in. He seemed fairly unflappable. "What about shutting down the engines?"

"The nuclear reactors?" Drake asked. "I can't reach any of the engineers down there. I don't know if any of them are alive, driven off, what."

"I'm an engineer," Martin said jauntily. "Corps of Royal Engineers."

Drake almost laughed. "That's great. But this isn't sapping, or pontoon bridges."

"Doubtless," Martin said. "But my degree is in nuclear. And I certainly know how a nuclear fission pressurized water reactor works. Enough to shut it down, anyway."

Drake gave him a look, half in awe, half in disbelief. He had no time to decide, so he just did.

"Okay, let's go. I'll see if I can get us a Marine escort."

But as he turned toward the ladder, a sailor came running up it, from the Launch Ops room. "Commander! Incoming aircraft, twelve o'clock." He pointed over Drake's shoulder out the porthole. *Oh, shit*, Drake thought, stepping outside again. It was the C-2A Greyhound – back from inserting the USOC team in Chicago. And here to land, refuel – and return to extract the team.

Without it, there would be no extraction. And no extraction, no cure. No cure, no last hope for humanity...

Drake cast his eye over the manic flight deck – flames, debris, living, dead, and undead.

The plane buzzed around in an arc.

The pilot no doubt seeing the same thundering shit-storm below.

STREET BATTLE ROYALE

For this mission, Ali had selected as her primary weapon a Mk 12 Special Purpose Rifle – what was sometimes called a "designated marksman weapon." Not quite a sniper rifle, it was still very effective out to 600 or 800 yards (more like 1,000 with Ali driving). And not quite an assault rifle, it was still very handy when things got hairy up close and personal. It looked like an M4 on steroids, with a large scope, bipod, suppressor, straight magazine, and air-cooled upper receiver. It allowed Ali extreme flexibility – and allowed her to carry only one rifle, which was much more pleasant when jumping out of a plane.

With one eye to the Mk 12's 3.5-10x tactical day optic, and the other wide open, she tried to track targets. There still were quite a few of them. And, moreover, they were just *jackrabbit sons of bitches*. At first, they seemed to take it easy and stagger around like your normal workaday Zulus. But when one of them got a whiff of Homer on the ground, or caught wind of Ali's shots chugging from up above, they just went batshit crazy – moving a hundred miles an hour, jigging, wheeling, and finally *leaping* upon their prey – whether that be Homer down below, or the bottom of the 'L' platform where Ali was laying up.

She took a headshot on one that hadn't been activated yet. Cake. But then her other eye registered movement, two of them, coming in fast. She swiveled on her bipod trying to track. The first one she caught with a round in the center of mass – and this slowed it enough for her to *just* make a headshot. The second got by her totally. She could hear Homer's rifle going cyclic down below.

So far, two had totally slipped by both Ali's overwatch and Homer's patrolling of the ground below, coming from unexpected directions. And these ones had enough vertical juice to leap up and *grab* the bottom of the train platform. Both had been killed while trying to haul themselves up – one by Homer below, one by Ali above (with her sidearm). Luckily, having to climb had the effect of both slowing and steadying them.

But it wouldn't take too many more of these to swarm up, over, and across the platform, overwhelming Ali's position. And with overwatch gone, Homer would probably go down shortly after. That level of threat wasn't here yet. But Ali could see it coming, as the bastards multiplied. She was starting to think very seriously about moving inside the target building, and up top with the others. But Handon hailed her first.

"*Ali, Handon, how copy?*"

"Ali copies, send it."

"*Yeah, stand by. We're coming to you.*"

She blinked heavily. "Repeat your last."

"It's a dry hole. We're all moving overground to a secondary target. Down to you in five mikes."

Ali swallowed heavily, squared herself up – and addressed her full attention to trying to clear the street for her team, before they were all down and neck-deep in it.

* * *

Homer had no problem operating on his own. SEALs were a little more comfortable in pairs (swim buddies and all that), but they were totally modular, configuring into groups of one, two, or four, up to multiple platoons of 16. The problem today was that these Foxtrots were *fast*. And having someone to watch his back, literally, would have been very welcome right about now.

The issue wasn't so much dealing with the handful that got curious and made their way up the street toward him. The problem would be arousing the interest of those thousands most likely behind them. Every time he or Ali fired a shot, and every time one of the soulless had time to emit a moan in response to prey, it increased the likelihood that the dam would burst.

And then they'd be awash in the three million missing Zulus. Or perhaps three million Foxtrots, God preserve them.

Correction: Homer, alone down on the street, would be awash in the three million.

He pictured himself being washed out to sea on a literal tide of the dead, like Noah in some horrifying Biblical Story/Zombie Apocalypse mashup…

* * *

In the end, Juice hadn't seen any reason to go looking for trouble. If the building they sat on top of was full of dead… well, that was a fantastic place for them, safe behind a locked door, and he and Predator would very happily leave them the hell alone. Seeming to validate this intuition, on his way back, he got his marching orders from Handon – or rather his lack of them.

"Yeah, we're gonna try and consolidate with Ali and Homer on the ground, and all move together to a secondary target site. You two take it easy for now. We'll figure out how to get you down off of there later."

"Roger that. Good hunting."

A few seconds later, he turned the corner into view of Predator, who was lying where he'd left him – and who of course had heard the whole exchange on his own team radio. He was also busy manufacturing an improvised splint, made up of a section of two-by-four which he'd snapped in half with his bare hands, and which he was now duct-taping to his fractured leg. Around and around he wrapped the heavy tape. The agony this cost him must have been soul-scraping. But he didn't make a sound, and only gritted his teeth in concentration.

"*Oh*, no, man," Juice said – knowing this was useless even as he tried it. Pred didn't even look up. So Juice just sighed and started gathering up their gear. When Pred was up on his feet – or rather on one foot, the other stuck out like a drumstick, silently belying the torment this too must have caused – the two hobbled together back to the access door. Before Juice could address the matter of breaching it, Pred shredded the lock with a buckshot round from the Metalstorm shotgun slung under his rifle.

And without a pause, he went straight into the darkness ahead, firing and cursing, and hobbling on one agonizing drumstick.

Juice took a breath and went in straight behind him.

They would simply fight their way down. Hardly for the first time.

* * *

After Alpha hit the ground, consolidated, and got moving, it quickly became obvious where the Foxtrots were coming from.

They were coming from exactly where Alpha was *going* to. With each block the team covered, the opposition they faced increased. It seemed that every Foxtrot they dropped brought four more. And they were expending a lot more ordnance per kill than any of them were accustomed to, so difficult were the damned shots. It was truly turning into some *Black*

Hawk Down shit. Including the dwindling ammo.

All eight of them had hit the street at the same time – Ainsley, Handon, Pope, and Henno down from the target building... Homer half-catching Ali as she dropped by her fingertips from the platform... and Predator and Juice stumbling out of the building across the street. The storm was well over now, but the streets still slick, and the sky still a low and oppressive gray.

Synchronized movement had long been part of their playbook. They were more like a dance troupe than shock troops sometimes – even if Juice and Pred were cutting in today. When Ainsley and Handon saw them, they just shook their heads. Ainsley briefly considered trying to order them back. Handon instantly knew that to do so he'd have to *fight* Predator. And they all had more than enough fight on their hands as it was.

Ali had rigged up a nylon sling to help elevate the barrel of her weapon. Pope and Handon passed a few rifle magazines over to Homer, who was already running low. Ainsley got a bearing and took the lead. And they all moved out.

Bounding overwatch, the old fire and movement routine when moving to contact, was right out. Now it was just haul ass – and make shots on the hoof. It's only with tens of thousands of hours of training and drilling in close quarters battle (CQB) that soldiers can make shots on moving targets, while also moving themselves. (While a staple of blustery Hollywood dreck, it's actually one of the most difficult feats of arms imaginable.) Luckily, every member of Alpha had that level of training – plus thousands of hours shooting in operational situations.

And this was a good thing – because battling through swarms of Foxtrots, they discovered, was like being tossed into the Velociraptor pen. They came from everywhere – but more often from nowhere, fell flashes of mottled flesh, bared teeth, and cracked, filthy, slashing nails. Where they got the energy for this, none of the living could imagine. Then again, the dead seemed to violate most of the known laws of biology.

The eight moved in a staggered line, each responsible for an overlapping sector, 360-degree zombie warfare. Ali, with her superior vision and situational awareness, spotted two of them coming dead from the front ("zero angle on the bow" as Homer would put it), at full speed, and well before Ainsley did. She steadied her rifle on her half-dead left arm. She fired twice. Both went down. Their dead-on approach did mean they jigged less.

As they passed a crap-strewn alley on their left, Pope swiveled to cover it. But he was a little too close to its mouth, and they were moving too fast, and two of them blasted out and were on him before he could bring his rifle around. The three figures tumbled into a maelstrom of living and dead flesh, Pope's rifle wedging up in between them and clanking on the blacktop. Henno reacted and turned in to help. But

Pope already had two knives out, one in each hand. In less than a second of flashing butchery, one dead arm had been cut loose, a hand off, and two brainstems speared – one from above, one from behind. Henno pulled Pope to his feet, and they both accelerated onto the back of the column.

Ainsley clocked all this. *"How's he look, Henno?"*

Henno eyed Pope up as they ran. There was a fair bit of gore on his chest and left thigh. But, in addition to being bite-proof, the suits were pus-proof. "He's good," Henno said. *He'll want to be hosed off later,* he thought, *but we can deal with that if we live long enough...*

After three frantic blocks south, Ainsley led them in a jog to the right, one block west. Without any kind of overhead surveillance to find them the clearest route, Ainsley was just going full out. Keeping the turns down to two, but otherwise just going hard and fast.

Handon, still tail-gunner Charlie, actually felt like he was having an okay day of it. He sure wouldn't want to be as dinged up as Predator or Ali and try this. But for his part, and with the spiritual kick he got from dire peril, he was having a good outing. He spared some of his attention for the sectors of the wounded, in case they got overwhelmed. But otherwise, it was a little like a day on the CQB range – motorized pop-up targets zanging up and racing by, or lurching straight at him. The cardboard versions wouldn't chomp your neck, killing you and then

118

reanimating your corpse as a monster which would then kill your friends... but otherwise. His adrenaline was up. He just had to look out for his people. It was complete madness. But in a good way. He was in the zone, in a perfect state of flow.

But just when he was getting sanguine, that's when he saw one *fall* on top of Homer up ahead. As Handon moved to react, a second one came out of a window, right on his arm. *Fuck*. Wrestling is not a recommended tactic for zombie warfare – and neither Homer nor Handon had Pope's laser-gun knife skills. Homer let his rifle fall on its sling, and came around with his boarding axe, putting it straight through the mottled and worm-eaten face of his attacker. Handon held onto the pistol grip of his rifle, while drawing his second .45 and rapid-firing point blank. The zombie's head turned into a canoe, and brain matter and black pus splashed Handon's face shield. While regaining his feet and resuming the mad run, he pulled the fouled plastic mask off and tossed it. Dripping with infectious material, it was more of a hazard now. Though the next such splash might be lethal, ruining Handon's good day out – and switching his allegiance for good.

Thank God, they were finally approaching the Hyatt from the rear. Through the cross street, they could make out the twin cylindrical towers of the riverside Chicago Mercantile Exchange Center.

Virtually only the towers themselves were visible.

Because the lower stories were encased in a

writhing skirt of meat – dead but animated bodies piled dozen upon hundred, clawing to get deeper in, climbing to get higher, pulling off pieces of themselves and others, wriggling like a plague of maggots in some Lovecraftian hell.

Ainsley actually had to swallow the contents of his stomach back down, when he caught sight of it. Now the entire group caught the stench. It smelled like what it was – an enormous pile of thousands of rotting dead bodies. And the dead out on the edge were starting to catch scent of the living. *Fuck the hotel entrance*, Ainsley thought, shooting out a large pane of groundfloor glass, and leading the group straight inside the hotel at a gallop. In the rear, Handon turned around and started moving backward, making rapid single shots on the scores of swarming, enraged, starving, hyper-powered soulless, who were now moving to follow them in.

Within thirty seconds, they found a service stairwell. *Down, fuck it, down*, Ainsley thought. They were so close – but playing it way too close to the bone. There were also a few strays inside the building, in their own patch of turf, converging on the noise. The operators put them down in close quarters in whatever way seemed to hold most hope of keeping themselves on their feet. But behind them, through the shattered glass, a much greater mass of undead were sluicing into the building, filling up the space behind Alpha like air into a vacuum.

Juice spared a lightning look back to make sure

his battle buddy was still with him. He caught a strobe light flash of Pred flyingly unscrewing the suppressor off the end of his rifle barrel and letting it fall. Without asking, Juice instantly knew why: the suppressor slowed rounds, and Pred wanted his full muzzle velocity; also, it was already so tight in here that bringing your weapon to bear was tricky – the shorter the barrel length the better; and, finally, who the goddamned hell else was the noise going to attract? The entire former population of Chicago already seemed to be on them. Juice made a mental note to take his off, if he happened to get two seconds to rub together at any point during the rest of his life.

Which floor? Which fucking floor? Ainsley gritted his teeth. There were several below-ground levels, and he didn't have any better intel than "in the basement." *Fuck it*, he thought – *in for a penny, in for a pound*. He'd take them all the way to the bottom. If there was no secret door there, well, it was a perfect place to be buried.

Buried under the weight of thousands of dead.

"*Room clearing drill!*" he shouted across the squad net. It was the quickest way to scour every part of every room on the level. "*Looking for a secure door!*" Out of habit, he instantly went to the heavy side – the one with a pair of Foxtrots coming to life and leaping down the dark and dirty corridor. Indoors, thank fuck, they couldn't dance around so goddamned much. On the other hand, it was so tight they were on you in fractions of a second.

Handon took the light side – but it didn't stay that way long. He knew the other six would be dynamically making decisions about movement and fire, based on a hundred factors, including visible opposition, the layout of the structure, and what the guy ahead of him was doing. They flowed through and across and around the floor in a slithering flash, dropping attackers at fast-forward speed, passing in full view of other operators and holding fire, a supremely controlled chaos. This was what they were very, very best at.

It was only twenty seconds later that Homer announced: *"Found it! North edge, beyond the boiler room."* By the time the full group converged, Homer had the dummy code entered and the door open. But by the time they were all through it and inside, the great mass of dead were on them.

Juice and Predator, the two biggest men (and Predator was strongest, even on one leg), pushed on the door with all their strength, while the others fired out the slit into the mass of hissing mouths and undulating dead flesh outside. Finally, Pope got a tiny look at open air and tossed two grenades through. "Frags up!" he shouted and everyone hunkered down. The explosions didn't even kill the ones against the door, shielded as they were by the bodies of others. And the sheer mass of corpses was too much now – animated or not, they were keeping this door open.

While the others held the dyke, Handon scouted

frantically forward. Dim blue LEDs illuminated the floor – it was only twenty meters of corridor, running alongside a scooped-out enclosure of chugging machinery, which Handon clocked as a large diesel generator, and then terminating in another door at the end. This one was steel, and solid, and had no keypad or reader. The long lever handle wouldn't budge – locked from the inside. *Fuck.* Handon was reaching for a shape charge to blow it when his peripheral vision registered movement. He came up with his sidearm in a blur – but only found himself aiming at a mini-CCTV camera above and in the corner. Its active red LED was lit. And Handon was sure it had moved.

Fuck it, he thought again, holstering his pistol and pulling out the shape charge. *No time.*

But then… the door simply opened. A youthful man with short dark hair and brown-framed eyeglasses stood behind it. For a quarter second neither seemed to know what to say. Then they both spoke at once:

"Get in!" shouted the man.

"Make way!" shouted the sergeant major.

BENEATH THIS DEAD EARTH

Juice and Pred stayed in the rear, now covering the fighting withdrawal. They stepped backward down the dark hallway, Pred dragging his badly swollen and immobilized leg, both of them firing incessantly. They got in sync – each reloading at the midpoint of the other's magazine, empties dropping out with a scraping sound, and hitting the cement floor with a clunk. Ejected shell casings hit the walls and the floor with a tinny sound. And the rifles roared.

The dead flew at them with ravenous single-mindedness. None of these could have fed in months or years. All were driven to frenzy – though whether by hunger, or merely hunger to infect, was a question no one had time for. As they leapt forward, levering by the destroyed ones in front with their stringy arms, Juice actually thought they might start using the walls and ceiling to come at them. It was all already *way* too much like the teeming-horde scene from *Aliens*...

As they neared the back end of the corridor, Pred emptied the remaining four buckshot rounds from his underslung Metalstorm launcher – then jammed in a pack of five high explosive (HE) rounds. Juice gave him a look – in this enclosed area, the overpressure caused when the rounds exploded could *seriously* fuck them all up. As in kill them. But there was nothing else for it. As things stood, the horde was too close, virtually on top of them – the dead would be on the inner door at the same time the last humans tried to go through it. Then they wouldn't be able to close that one, either – and then all of them would be doomed.

As Pred slammed shut the receiver on the five-round munition tube, an unseen hand grabbed his collar and pulled him backward. He almost tumbled ass over teakettle, and as he staggered backward, his assailant pulled his rifle out of his hands. It was Ainsley. He pivoted and gave Juice a mighty shove with his strong right arm, then turned away, into the horde. Pred and Juice tripped over each other – falling right through the doorway and into the others inside.

The first HE round went off only a few feet down the corridor. It ruptured the eardrums of both Juice and Pred, and sucked the air out of the lungs of everyone behind. The overpressure also slammed the heavy, handleless door closed with a whump.

Behind it, four more explosions sounded dully.

* * *

"Simon Park," the young man said. He was trembling badly. "Doctor Simon Park."

Handon took his hand. Even as completely unhinged as the world had gone... it still must have been a bad shock for this guy to find seven heavily armed commandos, dripping blood and zombie gore, suddenly standing in his secret bunker. "I was expecting someone older," Handon said.

"Yeah, I get that a lot." Park pointed at the heavy inner door. "Your… your friend… Jesus…"

"He's gone," Handon said, repeating a scene he'd acted out a hundred times. He turned slightly toward the others. "And we pick up his banner and carry on. While there's breath in our bodies." The others nodded. There hadn't been any real need to say it. But it served as a passing of the torch of command. Ainsley had made his choice, spending his life gloriously. And they were all alive because of it.

Predator turned away and staggered into the main room, looking for and finding a couch. Blood dripped from his ears. "Not sure there *is* breath in my fucking body…" he said, too loud, and collapsed. Juice followed to look after him.

* * *

It was an underground complex of more than twenty rooms. Several of them, most of the larger ones, were filled with computers, desks, network gear, phones, and large display screens. Most of the rest were one type or another of living quarters – bedrooms, bathrooms, a kitchen, an enormous supply closet (really a mini-warehouse), and the large living room in which Alpha, or the remainder of it, sprawled out now. They peeled off sweaty assault suits – several of them after being hosed down in the shower – dropped their heavy rucks on the floor, shrugged out of assault vests, unchambered and safetied weapons, tightened bandages, and chugged down bottles of water.

Park talked directly to Handon, who was also gearing down. The others listened.

"They built all this after 9/11," Park said. "When they saw how long the New York Stock Exchange was out of action after the attacks, they decided to make sure they could continue trading through any kind of disaster. Natural or man-made."

"Yeah," Handon said, sitting and loosening his assault boots. "We saw your e-mail."

The young scientist's eyes went wide. "You were at NeuraDyne?"

Handon nodded. "That's what we came for. Your research data."

"So… there's someone left out there? Somewhere?"

"Britain. It stood when everyplace else fell. Listen – how long was this bunker designed to hold out for?"

"Three months. But that was with a full staff of traders, techs, managers, executives – everyone vital to operating the Exchange. With just one man, me, the food and water looks like lasting for years. As for the diesel generator… well, I conserve power, and only run it when the batteries need topping up. I'm about halfway through the fuel."

Handon perked up. "Juice," he said. "Get to the trading room. Get on their radio set, if they have one. Or try to hook one of our radios into an aerial or repeater, if they've got that."

"On it," Juice said, rising with his ruck and striding out.

"Pope. Check the perimeter. Especially the other door, and outside via the cameras."

Pope nodded and glided out.

Handon slumped down a bit on the couch again, and pinned the young man with his eye. "And so where are all these people who are supposed to be here?"

Park shrugged. "They never turned up. I'm guessing the dead swept the trading floor before anyone could make it down here. It's just me."

"Well, bully for you," Henno said, levering himself up. "I'm gonna recce the kitchen."

"I'd murder a bacon sandwich," said Predator – who'd finally consented to taking a half gram of morphine sulfate. He lay diagonally on a large loveseat, taking up the whole thing.

"Okay. How do we get out of here?" Handon asked.

"I don't think we can. You must have seen – the building is literally covered with them."

"Why is that?"

Park shook his head quickly. "I don't know, not for sure. I think maybe it's because I'm the last living person in Chicago."

Ali snorted with laughter. "A LaMOE! We found one."

"What?" asked Simon.

"Never mind," said Handon. "How do the dead know you're in here?"

"That's been a matter of some speculation on my part. I thought maybe it was because of the toilet flushing. It would be the only one."

Homer looked up. "Where does your garbage go?"

"Um. I don't know. It gets sucked out a pneumatic tube, about once a week."

"That's probably it right there. It will have organic matter in it, and they'll smell it. Like ringing the dinner bell."

Handon nodded, looking intent, and looking like changing the subject. "Your research... Have you cured the plague? *Do you have a vaccine?*"

Simon drew breath. "Yes and no."

Handon worked to swallow his irritation. He refrained from pointing out that what they'd all just gone through to get there probably at least merited a straight answer. "*Go on.*"

Park nodded. "I don't know how much you know about vaccine research – or care to. There are several types of novel vaccine strategies that presented themselves as possible candidates for the zombie plague – for a double-stranded RNA virus. I focused my work on a possible recombinant vector vaccine. Using data from the dsRNA interference technique we worked out, I was able to combine the physiology of one microorganism and the DNA of the other, creating immunity against an organism with as complex an infection process as this one has."

"So does it work, or doesn't it?"

"Yes," Park said, finally. "It works against the early samples of the virus I have here. But the virus is clearly mutating. Hell, it's mutating in here, in test tubes, in isolation. But out *there*..." and he tossed his head toward the steel doors. "With two years, and the whole world as a breeding ground... look, I've got a lot of external cameras. And I can see the changes in their behavior, even from in here. But I wasn't going to open that door, not just to get new samples. Plus... I didn't really think there was anyone left in the world to immunize..."

Handon blinked. "So you're saying it wouldn't protect anybody from the virus as it is today?"

"I believe it could be *made* to work on current strains of the virus. I'm sure of it. All I need is to understand which features of the virus are transitory, and subject to significant mutation – and which aspects are enduring. Look, all organisms have DNA that stays basically the same over time. I target my technique to *those* genes and, blammo, we've got a universal vaccine."

"Okay," Ali said, from across the room. "How do you find out which genes have endured?"

Park paused before answering. He looked like he was worried how his next statement was going to go over.

"I need patient zero."

Handon snorted, shaking his head mordantly. *Isn't that just like the ZA*, he thought.

With this, Juice returned to the main room.

"No go, Sarge. I've got long-range radio transmission capability. But it's like the *JFK*'s just not there. Or everyone on it's asleep... or dead."

Now Predator snorted. "I'm gonna take a shit."

Juice moved to help him up.

BEAR ANY BURDEN

Drake bounded down the stairs of the island to the *JFK*'s Ops room. "*Status!*" he bellowed.

One of the duty officers, puffy headphones on, answered, "It's the Greyhound. She's coming in on final approach, whether we're ready or not. Running on fumes, sir."

"Can you get her down?"

"It would help a lot if we controlled Pri-Fly," the officer said tightly, referring to Primary Flight Control, on the top level of the island. "But we can do it from here. Especially since we've got no choice…"

Just as Drake felt he was reaching maximum cognitive capacity, Master Gunnery Sergeant Fick stomped into the room, reeking of cordite, and streaked with soot and droplets of blood. His scarred and scowling face was a mask of frustration. "God*damm*it," he said, striding up. "Sir. Those bastards are dug in like Alabama ticks. I've got multiple casualties. And now my men are desperately needed to try and control this zombie outbreak. If we don't deal with that, we're all done for."

Drake remembered to draw breath. "And if we don't stop the ship from crashing into land, this vessel is done for… And, fuck me, if we don't refuel this plane to extract the away team, the human race is probably finished…" He felt as if his brain were stewing in its own juices. But he took another breath, mastered himself – and gave orders.

"Gunnery Sergeant Fick – redeploy all your men here to battle the zombies. *Get the outbreak under control – whatever that entails.* They fight as a team."

"Sir." Fick started to turn.

"But they fight without you. You're going with Martin and Wesley. You get them safely to the reactor room." Fick knew as well as Drake that this was a heavily armored, heavily restricted area dead in the middle of the ship. But he didn't seem daunted.

"And you, Commander?" Martin asked.

"I'm going to get that plane down – and, God willing, back up again." The others looked at him. "We might make it here, and we might not. But if we get that bird in the air, then at least those men in Chicago have a chance. And so does humanity."

He was already turning away toward the operator at the control station.

* * *

After dashing upstairs, leading his men as they withdrew and broke contact with the Zealots, and retasking them to assault the burgeoning ranks of zombies, Fick returned to the Ops Center and rounded up Martin and Wesley. He'd rearmed out of a weapons locker, 18 full magazines of 5.56 for his

M16. He gave four of them to Martin, who still had Drake's rifle, and who shoved them in his pockets. Nobody had any spare ammo for Wesley's pistol, so Fick gave him his sidearm, with two spare mags. He squared up and gave orders to his new two-man command.

"Listen up. We're going to be moving hard and fast – and fluid. *Stay on me*. Stop for nothing. Your sector will be everything between my eight o'clock and four o'clock – that's behind me. Okay? If you have to take a shot, take it with authority and move on. You should know whether a headshot is required. If you shoot a loyal sailor by mistake, that will suck for him, and also for you. But it doesn't matter. We are moving to save the ship. Everything else is secondary – including and in particular us. Understood?"

The two Brits nodded.

Fick paused and seemed to grow thoughtful, then looked to Martin. "Well, not you, actually. You're the only son of a bitch who knows how to stop this crazy thing. Okay – on me! *Go, go, go!*"

The three of them spilled down the exterior stairwell of the island and onto the flight deck.

MARSOC Marines were already pushing out a perimeter. The dead were mostly down; and any sailors who might have been Zealots were suddenly acting like they weren't. (*One problem with a fucking mutiny*, Fick thought. *No real way to tell who's who...*) The three crossed a hundred meters of deck in a tight knot, then descended through the same hatch from which Martin and Wesley had so recently been greeted by fire and death.

Fick had his rifle pulled in tight to his shoulder, eye down to his EOTech holo-sight, swiveling at the hips, covering almost 180 degrees. *Every Marine is a rifleman*, they say. The other two did their best to stay close behind him.

And to make sure no one else did.

* * *

"You can *do* this," Drake uttered into the desk mic, leaning in over it. He was talking to the Greyhound pilot still circling above. "Arresting wires are up. And the deck is mostly clear. You're just going to have to catch the first wire. It's the only way you'll have enough clear deck to stop."

"*Copy that*," said the Navy pilot, perfectly poised and professional, as military aviators tend to be even in the most nerve-shredding circumstances. "*We're coming down one way or another. State zero plus zero-one to splash.*" This meant he had *one minute* of fuel left. "*But negative on deck landing. Seas are choppy – and if I go for the first wire, and the boat rises so much as two feet on a swell, we'll be eating stern. No, we're going to punch out and ditch it.*"

Drake jammed the transmit button. "*Negative, NEGATIVE.* Be advised – you are the *only* aircraft with the range to extract our team in contact. You are going to put that aircraft on the goddamned deck, we are going to tank it, and you are going to go get those men. Acknowledge!"

There was only the shortest pause on the other end.

"Aye aye, sir. We are inbound on short final."

Drake swatted the desk mic away from him, and it tumbled over.

He stepped out onto the balcony to check their position in the water.

North America was coming at them *way* too fast.

* * *

Fick took a round right between his shoulder blades, luckily in the ceramic plate in the back of his tactical vest. He spun on a dime and snap-fired one into the head of the Zealot behind them. A dead man lurched out of a cabin and fell on the man he'd just shot. Fick drilled it in the head.

He gave Martin and Wesley a look like: *What the fuck are you guys doing back there?*

But the passageways were narrow and twisting and dim, and very perilous. And despite being responsible for the Marine's back, they couldn't really keep their gaze turned around behind them. They were simply moving too fast. Fick did a lightning tactical reload and took off again. The other two dashed off in pursuit before he got out of sight.

They reached another ladder and descended. And

again. This new level looked deserted.

But when they got in the vicinity of the reactor, they quickly determined that it hadn't been taken by the Zealots.

It had been taken by the dead.

At least they won't know how to sabotage it, Martin thought mordantly.

The three of them spread out and started trying to clear the area.

Now, this, Wesley thought, almost happily, *I know how to do.*

Zombie fighting. It was becoming old hat for him now.

* * *

A carrier landing deck has four arresting wires, one of which a pilot must snag with his tailhook in order to bring his aircraft safely down and to a stop – on a strip that would otherwise be far too short for it. There are four wires because they are damned hard to hit, more so in rough seas. And even more so with a three-way mutiny and zombie battle going on all over the ship.

Pilots almost always go for the third wire – because the first two are uncomfortably close to the edge. Undershoot one of those, or have the ship rise on a wave, and you'll crash into the stern. But a bunch of even worse alternatives were making this one look pretty appealing. The pilot caught the first wire, on his first pass – which was good because he wasn't going to get another one. The bird screeched to a halt amidst clouds of white smoke. Deck crew dashed out to assist the pilot, secure the plane, and start the refueling.

The two pilots came tumbling out the cabin door, helmets still on, looking in every direction like they were in a fright house – which they were. Fires still burned, shots rang out, and the dead could still be heard to moan, amidst the screams of men. They raced through smoke to the island, just to take shelter until the Greyhound was ready to launch again.

They moved like men being chased.

* * *

Okay, Wesley mentally amended, turning a corner with his pistol held outstretched in both hands. *Maybe not exactly old hat.* In fact, he'd never fought zombies in what was basically a dungeon.

He heard shots ring out periodically – the hard snaps of the 5.56mm assault rifles. He hadn't fired his pistol yet. He was responsible for clearing the area closest to where they'd come in, on the fore side – which was basically already clear. Martin was aft. And Fick was right in the reactor center. Wesley thought maybe their shots had drawn them all from the entire deck.

"*Wesley!*" He jumped three inches at the sound of his name echoing down the deck.

"Yes!" He craned his neck, and peered down the hall.

"*Are you clear th—*" A gray face resolved out of the darkness, four feet in front of his head, mouth open, arms outstretched, and translucent eyes shining. It was on him in a fraction of a second. Wesley brought his handgun up and triggered off four rapid rounds. They caught the dead sailor across the chest and midsection and knocked it back a foot – enough room for Wesley to master himself. And make the headshot.

"*Wesley! You there?*"

He shook his head to clear it. His mouth was almost totally dry, and his voice cracked when he tried to yell back. "Ye— yes. I think I'm clear."

He stepped over the twice-dead corpse, and ran to the sound of the others. By the time he arrived, Martin was bringing down first one reactor and then the other.

"Starting a nuclear reactor is quite complex," he narrated, moving from one station to the other. "And running it in production can be demanding, and dangerous. But the designers and manufacturers make shutting them down pretty easy." He used a key to open up a covered switch. It read "Emergency Shutdown Enable". He flicked it. Then he pulled a large, conspicuous, two-stemmed red lever on the wall.

"For reasons that might be guessed."

* * *

Drake was debriefing the two Greyhound pilots when he felt it fading away beneath them – the immensely powerful rumble that always seized the ship when she was underway, the thrum of the enormous engines. He stuck his head out the door. The wind was slowing. And the rate of their approach toward the spit of land started to slow.

But he didn't think it was slowing enough.

Never mind, he thought. He looked to the fuelers out by the plane, with their enormous articulated hoses, and the hazy penumbra of jet fuel vapor around them. He caught one's eye. The man gave him a thumbs-up. Drake ducked back inside.

"Gentlemen," he said. (Naval aviators were always, by proclamation, officers and gentlemen.) "You're good to go." The two rose in their flight suits and followed him out. Drake stopped on the second-floor balcony and watched them descend. They hit the flight deck and began to trot out toward the waiting aircraft.

And then something else caught his eye. No, he heard it first.

It was one of the three enormous deck-edge elevators, which were used for moving aircraft from the hangar deck up to the flight deck and back down again. Drake racked his brain for why one of these would be coming up. God knows they weren't scheduled to move any aircraft.

And then he saw. The elevator was covered with the dead.

Scratch that, there were a few living – mostly being fed on. Those were probably the ones who had actuated the elevator – using it to try to escape. But they hadn't gotten away quickly enough. Fast these elevators were not, and the dead had followed them on. Now it was a hydraulic charnel house. As it came into view, almost level with the deck, one of the living tried to haul himself over to safety – but was pulled back down from behind. As the platform came level, the dead there sensed the living on the flight deck.

And they all clambered out.

Shots began ringing and zipping – from both the loyalists, and the Zealots on the bridge.

Drake turned his gaze to the two pilots. They were *very* aware of what was going on – and now running flat out toward the (relative) safety of their aircraft. Drake ducked back inside, grabbed a rifle and went back out. All was madness – even more confused and panicked than it had been before. He made out the aviators – still on their feet. He looked for zombies.

Oh shit, he thought, seeing one that had clocked the pilots. He tried to draw a bead, through the roiling smoke, through the adrenaline, over the rolling deck. He fired – missed. Fired and missed again. Now the zombie reached the co-pilot, and grabbed with both hands and bit. *Fuck!* Drake fired again. The zombie's head turned to spray. The co-pilot fell down along with it. The pilot, who had been looking back, turned forward again, put his head down, and reached the plane. He climbed in and slammed the door behind him.

"Thank God," Drake whispered. And thank God it only took one to fly that thing. And mostly thank God that, with no men or equipment aboard, that plane could get off the deck without the catapult. Both prop engines spun up, and the pilot rolled it out, right over the wheel blocks. He turned, taxied, looking for a clear lane down the deck. He didn't quite find it and so instead went straight into two zombies, shredding them through the propellers. He accelerated rapidly after that, dropped off the edge of the deck, rose again, and turned his nose inland.

Drake lowered his rifle and smiled.

The horrifying, cosmic grind of the bottom of the ship smashing and scraping into the sea bottom stopped everyone in their tracks. Drake's smile melted away.

The *John F. Kennedy* had floundered.

They were run aground.

CONTACT

Down in the basement bunker, deep beneath undead Chicago, Handon re-tasked Juice. Instead of helping Predator take a dump, he went to work with Dr. Park in trying to transmit all of his research data out of there and back to the *JFK*. The two had disappeared to the trading room, carrying Park's laptop and the team's long range radio transmitter. Now they returned to the living area where the others were tabletop-gaming ideas for getting out of the Exchange Center alive. Which they'd actually only need to bother with if they managed to contact the carrier and arrange their air extraction.

"No dice, boss," Juice said. "I don't think anyone's receiving on the data channel, either. At least, I got no acknowledgement. There's no way to be sure any of it went out. I'll keep trying. But right now it's looking like we're just going to have to walk this stuff out of here."

Handon took this in. He was used to missions where things frequently went from bad, to worse, to "you're fucking kidding me." But now, not only were they buried under a sea of the living dead – but so was the last, best hope for the world, a chance at a cure. And so now the operators' fates were tied to that of every other living person left on the planet. And Handon needed to do what he'd done so many times before: dig down deeper.

It just felt like there wasn't much left down there anymore.

Well, he thought, *it's just one more goddamned thing. And it's not like it's the end of the world…* This last thought amused him and raised his spirits. Also, he remembered, twenty minutes ago they thought they were all dead. Now at least they were safe in this bunker. For a while.

"What's that smell?" It was Park, looking around, and looking worried.

Then Handon noticed it. "Smells like engine exhaust… CO_2."

Juice stepped over to an air vent. "Yep. Coming from here."

"The diesel generator, out in the hall," Handon said. "Could it be malfunctioning?"

Juice snorted. "What, after five HE explosions in close quarters, and now an army of smushed zombies pressed all around it? Yeah, maybe." He turned to Park. "Where does the exhaust from that thing normally go?"

"I don't know—"

"Never mind," Handon said. "Shut it down. Now!"

Park nodded and dashed off. When he returned, he said expectantly, "Done. Better?"

But it wasn't better. Now they could all smell acrid smoke. And within a few seconds, they could see it visibly drifting in through the vent.

"Too late," Juice said. "It must have shorted. And maybe sparked something flammable nearby…"

"Zombie clothing?" Ali suggested. "Or Ainsley clothing. What happens when it hits Ainsley's ammo, or grenades?"

"Forget the grenades," Juice said. "There's a whole depot of diesel fuel out there."

Handon went to the door and pressed his hand against it. It was stove-top hot. "Where's the other entrance to this place?"

"On the other side of the bunker," Park said. "But we can't get out that way either. It leads up into the Exchange. And the building's completely enclosed in dead."

"Fuck," Handon spat, looking around helplessly.

"*Mortem One, this is Grey Goose Zero. How copy? Mortem One, Grey Goose Zero.*" This leaked out of the radio earpiece hanging on Handon's chest. Everyone in the room heard it. Handon jammed the earpiece back in and pressed his transmit button.

"Grey Goose, this is Mortem One Actual. Interrogative – what is your location and status?"

"*Mortem One, Gray Goose. I am inbound for extraction point Alpha, Chicago Miegs Airfield. ETA 35 minutes. But be advised – I have just enough fuel to touch and go. After about one minute on the ground at engine idle, I will be at bingo fuel. So you had better be on the spot and ready to get out of Dodge. How copy, over.*"

Handon's expression stayed neutral. "Mortem One copies all." That was great – their ride was inbound on a totally do-or-die schedule. And there was still no way for them to get through the army of dead outside to the extraction point. Oh, and they also couldn't stay where they were, because the building was burning down.

"Fuck," he repeated.

A not-quite-muffled explosion rocked the back door, from out in the hall. Probably one of Ainsley's grenades. The smoke coming in through the vent grew thicker and darker.

"Fuck."

Now several people were saying it.

But everyone was thinking it.

* * *

Henno wasn't given to speechifying. But now he stood, picked up Dr. Park's laptop, pointed toward the back exit, and spoke.

"The man just outside that door sacrificed himself – and he didn't do it to save *you* lot. He did it for the whole world. For his children. So just maybe they'll have a world to grow up in. And we fucking well *will* get this vaccine out of here and back to Britain."

No one spoke for a second.

"He's right," Handon finally said. "So saddle up. Take everything. We're moving out."

"Where to?" Homer asked.

"Far side of the bunker for now – if the fuel tank out in that hall goes, I'm not sure I see the inner door holding. We'll think of something else from there."

"Hell," Predator said, levering his huge bulk off the couch with three limbs. "I'm not sure I see this side of the structure not collapsing…"

As the commandos began an accelerated process of strapping everything back on, Pope sidled over to Handon. "Quick word with you, Top?"

The two of them led the exodus down the hall, then stepped off alone into the kitchen, as the others filed by. Suddenly Handon noticed that Pope wasn't looking too good. He clocked the sweat beading on Pope's forehead. The temperature in the bunker was rising now, but was still relatively cool. And when Handon squinted, focusing on Pope's face, he saw the early signs – those tiny black lines spreading out from the eyes and the mouth, faint red spots around the face and neck, and that strange glazing of the eyes.

"Ah, shit, Pope," Handon cursed, shaking his head.

"Yeah," sighed Pope, flexing his right hand and peering at the white dots already appearing on his fingernails. Body proteins being destroyed.

Handon looked Pope straight in the eyes. "Why didn't you say anything?"

"I didn't know until just now. Thought I was still just out of breath. Something. But that roll-around, during the run here, must have splashed me. On a bit of mucous membrane probably."

Handon held the other man's eye. "Do you want me to do it? Or on your own?"

"Neither." Pope spoke levelly and carefully. He knew that there was no one else that he would have wanted to end it, but he had another plan. "Use me. To get out of here."

"How?" asked Handon.

"Diversion," replied Pope, nodding in the direction of their blocked exit. "Send me up out the main exit."

Handon frowned. "You can't. It's overrun up there. A mass of meat."

"No," Pope said, shaking his head. "The *outside* of the building's meat. But the inside, the trading floor and whatnot, I think has just got a few from the internal outbreak. The outer doors must have held. I saw it on the security cams. Maybe a few dozen wandering around. However, if I go up there and *open* the outer doors…"

Handon nodded. "Then the ones outside will pour in. And maybe the ones in our back tunnel, and clogging up the basement of the hotel, will follow them."

"Exactly. They'll follow the frenzy and decamp, giving the rest of you a way out."

Handon thought seriously about this. He didn't have much time to ponder, but it depended on the dead doing exactly as predicted, and they weren't always predictable.

"And what if they don't?"

Pope smiled. "Well, you'll have nearly a half hour to think up a new, better plan."

"Jesus." Handon shook his head – 98.5% of humanity dead, and yet they still managed to produce heroes like this one. Right now, though, Handon would have given all of those others to hang on to this one for even just another day. For two years they had been the only team in USOC – perhaps the only deployed military unit anywhere in the ZA – never to lose a man. Now they'd lost two in the space of ten minutes. If felt like the world, or what was left of it, or maybe just their little sane corner, was falling to pieces. Handon pushed the feeling away, shoving it deep down inside him.

"You're ready to do that?" he asked, knowing the answer already. It was a stupid question.

"Oh, yes." Pope held up his hand and showed Handon the lesion that had appeared on the back of it, a long thin line that had already turned black, the edges starting to seep and grow raw. "I'm on my countdown anyway, and I don't want to be around long enough for the bell to toll. Let's do this."

Handon paused for the briefest of moments, held Pope's gaze again, and then nodded.

"Okay," he said.

KI KEN TAI I-CHI ("SPIRIT SWORD BODY AS ONE")

Pope had a minute or two to prepare. He wiped his sword down with a soft cloth, then sheathed it again. He cleared the chamber of his assault rifle, reloaded it, and slung it across his back. Then he did the same with his sidearm, re-holstering it. He catalogued the magazines and grenades on his assault vest by touch, along with others on his belt and in thigh pouches.

Briefly, he'd tried to take off his bite-proof assault suit, and put it on Dr. Park instead. After all, the scientist was a lot more important now. Also, suddenly, getting bit was much less of a big deal for Pope. But the others wouldn't hear of it. They made noises about being able to perform close protection just fine, thank you very much. But to Pope it was transparent that they just refused to send him out to his end looking, for a Tier-1 operator, naked.

Now the others were milling around the far end of the compound, by the main door, which led up to the Exchange Center. Someone had gathered up four large fire extinguishers, both CO_2 and dry powder varieties. Handon and Park were checking video feeds – trying to clock the location of everything upstairs, and as much of their outdoor exfil route as they could see.

Very soon, it was time. Because there was no time.

Handon and Pope nodded at each other, as the door swung open.

Without looking back, Pope began the climb up. The stairwell was clear. When he reached ground level, he pulled his sword with his right hand, and opened the stairwell door with his left.

There were three there. Pope dispatched them methodically with the blade. Pivoting, lunging, and striking, using the footwork and combination techniques of kendo, the ritual movement of it all soothed him. He felt so much as if he were back in the dojo at Hendon with Ali. Those were beautiful times. Beautiful memories. He suddenly remembered what he'd overheard Ali saying, to Homer, on their flight in: something about looping through your whole life in the last second of your life.

Maybe he'd get to experience it all once more.

Emerging from his brief reverie, he moved out of the stairwell, stepped over the headless bodies, and made his way forward. Within a minute, he found the main lobby and atrium of the south tower. It was like nothing he'd ever seen – the dead outside blotted out the sky. Literally every inch of the two-story-high glass, from one end of the lobby to the other, was pressed with writhing, dead flesh. It was something beyond a horror show.

"Well, no time like the present," Pope said aloud to himself, then moved to take up a position a little further out in the middle of the lobby. He removed an HE grenade from his vest, pulled the pin with his teeth – then whirled suddenly at footsteps behind him. It was Ali.

And also Handon, and Pred, and Juice. And Henno and Homer. The whole team. They walked up to him in silence in a line, then split in two, and formed a loose ring around him.

"Okay," grunted Predator. "You gonna throw that thing? Or make me stand here all day?"

Pope smiled out loud, turned around, and gave the grenade an easy underhand toss over the main desk. It hit the outer glass wall, dropped, and rolled a foot or two. The short, percussive blast took out the glass panels above and to either side, and for twenty feet in all directions. And in came the dead with their own rumbling explosion of moans. They *literally* spilled in. And, in a frenzy, those that could still locomote rushed the circle of the living. As they approached, the operators could hear the moaning being picked up outside, and repeated down the block.

"FPF!" Handon barked. "Two volleys! On my signal!" Final Protective Fire – an unrelenting volley of full-auto and grenades, generally only used in the most desperate situations. When the dead were ten meters out and closing, Handon gave the signal. In a fraction of an instant, the whole room lit up with a galaxy of muzzle flashes, and explosions of grenades further out. Those with MetalStorm launchers fired all five rounds of HE or buckshot. Those without chucked hand grenades. Everyone emptied their magazines in seconds, reloaded, and went again.

After the second volley, the dead were piled up in a semicircle halfway to the ceiling. With little delay, the dead behind them could be heard scrabbling over the barricade of their fellows. Nothing slowed the dead. Nothing dinged their self-confidence. The dead didn't ruminate.

"*O-karada o daiji ni*," Ali said quietly, kissing Pope on the cheek as she passed him by. A beautiful Japanese phrase, it meant "take care of yourself." But, literally translated, it was "your body is precious." The others shook Pope's hand, nodded, or clapped him on the shoulder as they went by. Homer was last.

"I'll see you in the next place, my brother," he said, looking warmly into his eyes.

And Pope thought to himself: *I am a very lucky man. I am blessed.*

Then he gripped his sword, drew his sidearm, and turned back to face the room.

Time for one last dance.

SALVATION

Homer pulled the stairwell door closed behind him and raced down to keep pace with the others. Just as they were spilling back into the bunker, a terrible explosion rocked the walls and floor, and hot gases rolled over them in waves. Homer instantly knew it was the diesel fuel tank from the back hallway. He also knew something else: God was watching over them. Because that explosion, timed so perfectly, would have cleared out that hallway of the dead, both the animated and squashed varieties.

It cleared their escape path.

Now, if Pope's sacrifice worked, and Homer didn't doubt for a second that it would, those that had crushed down into the hotel after them, would be reversing course, and following the noise, and the smell, and the general frenzy toward the lobby of the Exchange Center across the street.

Homer let his rifle fall on its sling, hefted one of the CO_2 extinguishers and hauled ass through the bunker, knowing the others would be right behind him. Sure enough, the inner door was gone from its frame, and flame and smoke poured in from outside. Homer gave it a long rolling blast from the extinguisher, then paused a second to let the gases clear.

"Everyone ready to go again?" Handon barked. He had his left hand wrapped around the thin bicep of Dr. Park, who had his laptop bag slung around him, plus clutched in both arms. The others stood poised like sprinters at the starting line.

"'Til the roof comes off, boss," Juice said.

"'Til the lights go out," Ali added.

The lights in the bunker went out. *One down*, thought Ali, pulling down her NVGs.

Predator spoke in the dark, as he did the same: "'Til my leg give out, then."

"That'll be never," Juice said, coming up in the others' vision as a puffy fluorescent green.

Homer pulled his *shemagh* up over his face, hefted the extinguisher, and charged.

* * *

The group burst out into the street, after fighting through moderate opposition in the hotel. Pope hadn't died for nothing – most of the dead had withdrawn. Homer spared a look back up the cross street, where the Exchange Center had turned from a meat wall to a meat funnel, sucking in the dead from all directions. *God lets no one die in vain*, Homer thought. He then turned the opposite direction, east, and led the team in their last run.

Pulling up the rear again was Handon – who also rode herd on Dr. Park, shoving him, and his laptop, out ahead of him. As they took off, Handon spared one quick look at his wristwatch. They now had 21 minutes to get across town, down the lakefront, and out to the airstrip on Northerly Island. It was 2.6 miles, as Handon had earlier measured it. This required only 8-minute miles of them, slower than their conditioning runs, and would have been completely manageable – if they all didn't happen to be encumbered with weapons, armor, and ammo, plus fighting their way through an entire city of Fucking Nightmare zombies. Plus running for their lives. Also, there was zero leeway on the timing. It was sudden-death, do-or-die.

Predator mocked up a plummy English accent, and parroted Ainsley: "'Two-point-eight miles over surface streets. You'll hardly notice it.' Easy for that son of a bitch to say, he doesn't have to do it now." Henno made a mental note to kneecap Pred later, if they lived.

This time the running street battle was like their earlier one, only more so – plus at only 75% of their previous strength, and also with one helpless passenger. They all ran, shot, reloaded, stabbed, dodged, and parried. Every zombie in the city not already there was now clearly headed for the Exchange Center – which meant that every zombie between the airstrip and them was headed directly their way. They cut through them with whirling blades, and mag after mag of 5.56mm, 7.62mm, .45-cal, and shotgun shells. Some were starting to conclude it was easier to pulp and dismember them, than to make headshots on these jackrabbit sons of bitches. Or maybe they were just too tired now. They painted a rich black smear of zombie blood across the urban heart of Chicago.

As they finally emerged from the forest of buildings, spotting ahead of them the open expanse of Lake Shore Drive bordering the water, they were all sucking wind and critically low on ammo. But Chicago still had zombies to burn.

As he ran and changed out magazines, eyes and ears scanning in all directions for threats, Homer heard something from an unexpected direction: up. It was the prop-engine buzzing of the Greyhound, already banking and descending, coming in from over the broad expanse of the lake.

Thank fuck, Homer thought. He slightly startled himself with this, realizing he'd probably been hanging out with Brits, not to mention heathens, for too long now. He tweaked their path, toward the north end of the island, which connected with the mainland via a narrow spit of road and footpath. He gasped for air, and steeled himself to race the final distance.

Hope was dangerous. But there was no way to avoid it. The appearance of the plane was making all of them start to believe that they *just* might get out of this alive after all.

DAMNATION

"*No, no, no,*" chanted Major Lee Vesbost, sole surviving pilot of the Greyhound transport aircraft. Early forties, big lean frame, short curly hair, and wry manner, he was an extremely experienced naval aviator, with a variety of challenging flying assignments behind him. He hadn't gotten as far as he had by being a mushy-headed dreamer, or wishful thinker.

"No, no, no," he repeated, trying to hold the plane on the long banking track that would line it up with the long narrow grass edge of the island, which was formerly the airstrip. His words were now like a totemic incantation. They didn't mean anything, had no affect. He was just denying it, ritually.

The first two hours of the flight from the charnel house of the *Kennedy* had been fine. Of course, he had been equally horrified to lose his long-time co-pilot, as hc was blessedly relieved to get the hell out of there alive. It had been a terrifyingly close call, and of course only one of them had survived. But some unseen sniper had taken off the zombie's head, giving Vesbost the time he needed to hurl himself into the cabin. After that, finding enough clear deck to take off had been another miracle.

For that first two hours, he'd just focused on the flight and the mission. He had paused briefly to wipe off the viscous gunk that had splashed from the exploding zombie's head. It had only caught him on the shoulder. Mainly. He'd left it at that.

Including when he started getting headachy and dizzy later on. But when the fever hit him, he realized. But still he denied it. There was nothing else to do. He thought maybe he could bull through. Maybe the infection wouldn't take him. He was the only one left to fly the plane, to make the extraction. This simply couldn't happen to him.

The gray of the city and sky, and the steel blue of the lake, started to go hazy and dark in his fading vision. It all began to go out of focus. And holding himself up over the yoke and flight controls was becoming impossible. But he was beginning not to care about that...

Down he went.

* * *

Juice had Pred's arm over his shoulder now. How the man-mountain had just *run* nearly three miles, on a leg that was mostly lumber, was beyond him. He was physically failing now. But it was okay. They were going to make it. They were halfway across the land bridge to the island – and they could see the Greyhound lining up for approach.

Coming onto the island proper, they turned right – heading south down the grass strip and straight toward the descending aircraft. It drew them all on in those final 200 meters. But then a strange wobble appeared in its wings. And then its altitude dropped – too low, way too low. As Juice exclaimed aloud, "Oh, no, no, no – *no!*" the twin-engine plane plowed nose-first into the south edge of the island, coming apart in an ugly pirouette of dismemberment, wings and tail and fuselage and aileron separating, and then the fuel tanks went up in a pretty orange explosion. The sound of it, and warm wash of air, reached them a second later.

The group slowed to a trot, then a stop.

They turned back around.

Out in the open now, they could all see, literally plain as day, the hundreds of Foxtrots racing after them, lurching, sprinting, tumbling, ravening, rasping. They'd be across the land bridge in less than a minute.

The six commandos and one civilian stood in a loose knot, all trying to catch their breath.

"Swim for it?" Homer suggested.

"Fuck that," Predator said. "I'm exhausted. And they'll just follow us out."

"Plus there's nowhere to go," Henno added. "I'm with the big man. Let's finish it here."

Homer knew that he could, like any SEAL, swim any distance, however winded he was. But Henno was right. There was nowhere to go. And, even if there were, he'd much prefer to stay and die with his team. With his brothers.

They formed a skirmish line, bowing it at the flanks, some taking a knee, others laying out their few remaining magazines before them. Pred actually sat down. He grunted in satisfaction, the relief of taking the weight off. He swiveled his head toward the others. "And I don't want to hear any of that 'It's been an honor serving with you' bullshit, either."

He wouldn't hear it. They all knew it already. And nobody had to say anything.

"JFK Combat Control to Mortem One. Mortem One, how copy?"

Handon could hardly hear – the others had started shooting at the advancing horde, which was also moaning and shrieking. He pressed his finger to his earpiece and squinted in concentration.

* * *

Commander Drake sat in one of the swivel chairs in the combat control center, leaning back, radio headset on. It felt *good* to have taken back their bridge, the whole island in fact. And it had felt particularly nice to kill or capture what had to be most of the rest of the living Zealots. But he quickly realized he had little time for feeling self-satisfied. He had critically urgent things to do. He pressed the transmit button and hailed again – hoping against hope.

"JFK Combat Control to Mortem One. Mortem One, how copy?"

He released the transmit bar. Tapped his finger.

"Mortem One Actual copies, five by five." Drake sat bolt upright.

"Holy shit! Outstanding. Mortem One, what is your status? Do you have the mission objective? Have you been extracted?"

"That's affirmative on the objective. But negative on extraction. Grey Goose has splashed down. Repeat, Grey Goose is down. Total loss. Over."

Drake boggled. They got the vaccine? But the plane had crashed? How? He pressed the transmit button. "What is your intent, Mortem?" There was no answer for a second. Drake thought he could hear resignation in the silence. Not surrender, and not quite defeat. But definitely resignation – to approaching death. Drake began punching at a bank of touch screens, calling up a map, and sliding the display over across North America. "Mortem, how copy?"

"We're here," Handon's distant voice answered. There was firing, explosions, and moaning behind it. *"But probably for only another minute or two. Over."*

Drake pulled at the map and zoomed with two fingers, then zoomed out again.

"Handon, listen. You and your people need to get on a boat, and you need to get out onto Lake Michigan. How copy?"

"Copy that. You know where we might find a boat?"

Drake leaned forward, intense. "Handon, the whole leeward side of that island is one big marina.

162

Can't you see it?"

More silence. But this one had a totally different flavor.

* * *

Handon stood up to his full height. The others blazed away around him. Ali had gone dry, and was out front with her wakizashi, spinning and slashing. Homer was down to his SIG 226. Park cowered behind them all, beyond terror, watching death surround and fall upon them. Handon went up on his toes. Sure enough. Just over the hill. Fucking masts.

"*Displace!*" he hollered. "Everyone on me! *Go, go, go!*"

Predator didn't look like he wanted to get up, so Handon joined Juice in hauling him up by his elbows. In seconds, the whole group was tumbling east, over the hill, and toward the edge of the island that faced back toward the city. In seconds they saw it: row after row of smart wooden slat piers stretched out over the water, branching into individual berths for small boats. Most were empty. But at least a dozen vessels were still tied up.

"*Which one?*" Ali yelled. "*Cabin cruiser?*" She held her black blade and sprinted ahead.

"*No!*" yelled Homer. "The engine will never start! No time to get it running..." That they had no time was obvious from Homer firing over his own shoulder at the nightmarish pursuers who clawed at their heels. "Sailboat!" Homer scanned ahead, assessed the vessels in an instant – then holstered his weapon, put his shoulder down and sprinted ahead in a primal burst of speed, toward his chosen ride. By the time the others were all out on the pier, he had cut (not cast off) one of the two lines, leapt aboard, and was now cutting away the sail cover from the main mast.

Ali leapt aboard to help him. Handon shoved the scientist aboard, then joined the others in pushing out a perimeter to defend the dock. Sprinting corpses streamed down it, reaching them in seconds. They were shot or decapitated, and went in the water to either side, or piled up in front. Handon pulled his .45 and started firing, while he pressed his radio earpiece to hear over the moaning and gunfire.

"This is what you've got to do!" Drake was yelling, too – he could hear how frantic it was on the other end. *"You need to chart a course and sail north to Beaver Island. It's nearly at the top end of Lake Michigan. How copy?"*

"Copy that!" Handon dropped his mag out, slapped another one in, and resumed firing quickly but evenly. The Foxtrots kept coming. They climbed over the growing pile of those destroyed. They would never stop coming. Handon thought, *On any other day, sailing the length of Lake Michigan might sound like a pain in the ass...* "What do we do then?"

"There's a small airport on the island. There can't be too many dead there. By the time you reach it, I hope I'll have

worked out some way to extract you. A helo full of fuel, mid-air refueling then ditch the refueler. Something."

"C'mon! Board!" This was Homer and Ali, hailing the defenders. While Handon watched, Ali slashed through the last mooring line. The boat began to drift out. Homer was running up the mainsail. The wind of the lake was still blowing hard. They'd have to tack. But there was wind.

"Roger that!" Handon said, walking backward, reloading, and continuing to fire. The others were behind him, climbing aboard. Handon holstered his empty .45 and drew his own short sword. "Top!" Predator bellowed. "Fucking c'mon!"

Handon could sense his radio battery beginning to fade. They'd need that later.

"This is Mortem One Actual," he said, turning, running for the boat, then jumping five feet of open water onto the moving wooden deck. "Signing off for now…"

* * *

Commander Drake pushed away from the desk. He could hardly believe it, and whistled aloud. He heard steps, and Gunny Fick appeared in the doorway. The two Brits stood behind him. Fick saluted. "Commander. Captain Martin here requests permission to join the damage party ashore. Thinks just because he knows how to shut down a nuclear reactor, he can refloat a beached carrier."

Drake nodded. But instead of answering, he just stood and walked past the men out onto the forward-facing balcony. Craning his neck, he could see the security perimeter the Marines had set up – but not the men of the work parties underneath the overhang of the flight deck, who were assessing damage to the hull. Others, mainly officers, were trying to formulate a plan that might get the supercarrier off the sandbar, and back out to sea. Frankly, at this point, Drake wasn't at all sure it would be possible.

Then again, he thought, *I used to think it wasn't possible for the dead to walk the Earth.*

He also never thought this mission would succeed, or that any of the insertion team would survive it. For that matter, he'd never really believed the *Kennedy* would last this long into the ZA – never mind discover a whole nation of other survivors.

Hope had been beaten to within an inch of its life.

But it wasn't dead yet.

ARISEN, BOOK THREE - THREE PARTS DEAD

ABOUT THE AUTHORS

GLYNN JAMES, born in Wellingborough, England in 1972, is an author of dark sci-fi novels. In addition to co-authoring the bestselling ARISEN books he is the author of the bestselling DIARY OF THE DISPLACED series. More info on his writing and projects can be found at www.glynnjames.co.uk.

MICHAEL STEPHEN FUCHS, in addition to co-authoring the bestselling ARISEN series, wrote the bestselling prequel ARISEN : GENESIS. He is also author of the D-BOYS series of high-concept, high-tech special-operations military adventure novels, which include D-BOYS, COUNTER-ASSAULT, and CLOSE QUARTERS BATTLE (coming later in 2014); as well as the acclaimed existential cyberthrillers THE MANUSCRIPT and PANDORA'S SISTERS, both published worldwide by Macmillan in hardback, paperback and all e-book formats (and in translation).

He lives in London and at www.michaelstephenfuchs.com, and blogs at www.michaelfuchs.org/razorsedge.

Made in the USA
San Bernardino, CA
06 March 2016